Not The End and Not The Same

NOT ALONE
Novellas

Nicole,

You make the world better.

Gianna Gabriela x.o.

USA TODAY BEST SELLING AUTHOR
GIANNA GABRIELA

COPYRIGHT

Not Alone Novellas

Not the End & Not the Same

Copyright © 2020 Gianna Gabriela

ISBN Ebook: 978-1-951325-25-1

ISBN Print: 978-1-951325-26-8

All rights reserved. No part of this book may be reproduced or transmitted in any form, including electronic or mechanical, or by any other means, without written permission from the author. The only time passages may be used is for teasers, blog posts, articles, or reviews, so long as the work isn't being wrongfully used.

This book is a work of fiction. Characters, names, places, events, and incidents portrayed are solely from the author's imagination. Any resemblance to actual places, people, events, or other incidents is coincidental or are used fictitiously.

NOT THE END

NOT ALONE NOVELLAS, BOOK 1

Not the End

Sometimes the only choice you have is to stand up for yourself.

NOT ALONE NOVELLAS

GIANNA GABRIELA

Not the End

GIANNA GABRIELA

COPYRIGHT

Not the End

Not Alone Novellas (Book One) Copyright © 2018 Gianna Gabriela

ISBN Ebook: 978-1733995092

ISBN Print: 978-1721822225

All rights reserved. No part of this book may be reproduced or transmitted in any form, including electronic or mechanical, or by any other means, without written permission from the author. The only time passages may be used is for teasers, blog posts, articles, or reviews, so long as the work isn't being wrongfully used.

This book is a work of fiction. Characters, names, places, events, and incidents portrayed are solely from the author's imagination. Any resemblance to actual places, people, events, or other incidents is coincidental or are used fictitiously.

Editor: Lauren Dawes

Proofreader: Brandi Kennedy

Cover design & formatting: Lauren Dawes (Sly Fox Cover Designs)

DEDICATION

To all of you.
Yes, all of you.
All of you who are lost.
All of you who have struggled.
All of you who have suffered at the hands of others.
All of you who have lost yourselves in the journey of life. All of you who look in the mirror and don't recognize the person looking back at you.
Search for yourself.
Find yourself.
Love yourself.
It's not too late.
It never is.

PROLOGUE

I KNOW THIS EMOTION TOO WELL.

I've known Jake since elementary school. I remember seeing him sitting at a lunch table on his own, and feeling sorry for him, I left my own table to join him. I remember the look on his face when he saw that he wasn't alone anymore. I remember asking my mom to pack me a second set of chocolate chip cookies because he really liked them—he loved them, actually—and I wanted to make him happy.

In middle school, things changed. He started being noticed by the other girls. He was growing into a man; he captured other peoples' attention with his shaggy blond locks and baby blue eyes. I remember the first time he moved up in the social ladder. I was sitting at our usual table, waiting for him to arrive so we could go about switching and trading whatever lunch our parents had packed for us that day. Apple slices for carrots. Chocolate chip cookies for raisin ones. It had become our thing. I saw him enter through the cafeteria doors and my heart immediately began to beat faster. It always happened when Jake was around. I watched him walk in my direction, watched him smile when he noticed me. He was closing the distance between us when Janice Walcott got in his way—when she got in our way.

From that moment on, our table wasn't cool enough for him anymore. It stopped being our table. It was just mine. He sat with Janice and her friends. Eventually, her friends became their friends and my Jake became her Jacob. It wasn't until a few months ago that he first approached me again. The rumor was that Janice had cheated on him, so he ended it. The halls were reeling with the news that Mills High's power couple had split. Guys were lining up to ask Janice out, and girls had never really stopped trying to get their claws into Jacob when Janice wasn't watching.

"Hey." That was what he said after joining me at my table again for the first time in years—the first time someone else had sat at my table with me. That was all I needed him to say for us to return to the place we were at before everything...before Janice.

For three months he sat with me every day. Three weeks ago he asked me to prom.

I said yes.

"You look so pretty," my momma says the moment she sees me coming down the stairs.

"Oh mom, it's your job to say that," I tell her as I reach the final step.

"It is, but it's true. You're going to be the prettiest girl at the ball."

"It's Junior Prom, mom, not A Cinderella Story," I tell her, though it might as well be one.

I still can't believe Jake asked me out. Not even in my dreams would a guy like him look my way, especially with all the other girls pining over him. I can't believe he chose me.

"When's your date coming?" Momma asks, the camera already hanging from her neck, ready to take photos of her baby girl.

"I'm meeting him there," I answer. Her mouth opens with what I know will be a follow up question, and I brace myself to give an answer she won't be thrilled with.

"Isn't it tradition for the guy to pick up the girl? Or am I stuck in the past?"

I shrug. "They still do that, but he had something important to do today so he asked me to meet him there." She looks at me skeptically, but I assure her, "It'll be okay, mom. I'll just drive myself."

"I can drive you if you want."

"I think that may be worse than showing up on my own." I say, laughing as my mother joins me at the bottom of the stairs.

"Bummer! I won't be getting pictures of you both together."

I run my fingers through my hair, making sure it's smooth enough. "I'll make sure I get you a copy of the one we take when we walk in."

"Okay, but in the meantime, I won't let this camera go to waste. Go ahead, strike some poses, Dimah."

I decide to give my mother what she wants and pretend to be a runway model. Today, I'm feeling confident. Which makes perfect sense, because when the hottest guy—a senior football player—asks you to accompany him to prom, you can't help but get some pep in your step. Little old me, the envy of all the other girls.

A few dozen photographs later, I give my mom a kiss goodbye and head to my car. The rules are simple: no drinking, no driving, and no sex. But we all know what happens at prom, and if Jake asks, I'm not sure I'll say no. Who could say no to a tall, muscular, handsome man with baby blue eyes and blonde locks like Jake's? Certainly no one else would. So why should I?

Driving to Mills High takes a few minutes and after parking my car in the student lot, I give myself a once-over in the mirror. Looking back at me is the most basic girl you've ever seen: brown hair, brown eyes, brown skin —nothing special. But I guess I must be somewhat special to get a boy like Jake to look my way, don't I? I reapply my lipstick, open the door, and get out.

1

I, TOO, HAVE LOST ME MANY TIMES BEFORE.

Four Months later...

"What's a pretty girl like you doing smoking that shit?" a voice says from behind me. I roll my eyes. Maybe if I ignore it, it'll just go away.

"You know you don't have to ignore me, Emerson," the voice continues. I take another draw of the joint I bought off one of the jocks at the dance. I hold my breath, hold in the smoke, and wait until I have no choice but to let it out.

"That shit's bad for you," he insists, interrupting my high.

I finally turn to the owner of the judgmental voice, which belongs to the new quarterback of the football team. Lincoln. Aron Lincoln. "You're saying you don't smoke?"

"Hell no," he answers, disgusted.

Of course he doesn't. I mean, star football player—

who parties like no other and is known for getting anything and anyone he wants—doesn't smoke. How poetic. "Great." Another inhale. Hold. Release.

"Why are you out here and not inside?" he says, finally approaching me.

"I don't like dancing," I reply, hoping he sees that I'm not in the mood for whatever the hell this is.

"There's got to be more to it than that," he presses, only mere inches from me now.

"Why are you out here and not in there with the rest of your fans?" I let the judgment drip from my tongue. There's no holding back tonight—at least not at this moment.

"I don't like dancing either," he answers, his expression serious.

I burst out laughing.

"She smiles!" he says, laughing with me.

The smile leaves my face almost immediately. "Don't get used to it." No one should get used to anything.

"Wouldn't dream of it," he says, raising his hands—palms out—to me. The proverbial white flag. "You okay, Emerson?"

I drop the end of the joint to the floor and put it out with my foot. Bending over, I pick it up and toss it in the nearest trash can. "You keep doing that. You should stop," I tell him.

"Keep doing what?" he asks, his brows lifting as he leans against the nearby wall.

"Keep saying my name like you know me. Like you talk to me every day."

"And that's problematic because?"

"Because you don't...you don't know me at all." Not many people do.

"Would it be terrible to start now?" he asks.

"Yes." And that's the last thing I say as I walk away from the front door of the school and head toward the parking lot. I put my helmet on, mount my motorcycle, and turn the key. The engine comes to life with a roar. Kicking the peg, I accelerate and take off, leaving the night behind. No dance should have ended like this, but that's just my luck.

"How was the dance?" my mother asks as I walk in the door, sufficiently late enough to make her believe I stayed. If it wasn't for her insistence, I wouldn't have gone in the first place; in her defense, if she knew what I'd been through in the last few months, she wouldn't have pushed me.

"It was good," I respond. I tell myself that I'm doing a good job keeping up the façade, but my mother must be living under a rock if she doesn't realize it. I think she chalks it up to 'discovering myself,' which is how she's justified my opting for a motorcycle instead of a car. How she's justified my opting to go away for the entire summer instead of staying around the house. My losing weight. Wearing all black. Yup, apparently she thinks it's all normal.

"Good, sweetie. I'm glad you had fun," she responds, watching me with tired eyes.

I know she's been working late shifts at the hospital, been on her feet for too long, working herself to the point of breaking. But I also know she loves her job. "Yeah, me too. I'm really tired though, so I'm going to head to bed," I tell her.

"There's some food in the kitchen if you get hungry."

"Thanks, mom."

"Love you."

"Love you, too," I respond before taking the steps to my room two at a time. I open the door then shut it behind me. Kicking off my boots and then my jeans, I lie down on my bed, staring at the ceiling as the tears fall. I guess I just can't keep them at bay anymore. I guess nothing has changed—even though everything has.

Prom Night

I WALK THE SHORT DISTANCE TO THE MAIN ENTRANCE FOR prom. Everyone around me is dressed so beautifully and for once, I feel like I fit in. For once, in the last two miserable years of high school, I feel like I'm going to have a good time. I'm finally going to make some friends. Finally going to have my first kiss.

I enter the room with a giant smile lighting my face, the happiness I'm feeling seeping out. Jake said he'd meet me here. I take a look at my phone but find no incoming texts. No worries; he's probably already inside.

Walking by a few other people laughing and chatting about college and after-party plans, I head over to the photographer to have my junior prom photo taken—alone. But it's okay; maybe I can take one with Jake later. I'm sure Mom would appreciate one with me alone and one with the two of us anyway.

Jake and I.

Jacob Hastings and Dimah Emerson.

I smile at the sound of our names finally coming together.

In awe of the beauty, I enter the elaborately decorated room the prom committee has spent weeks working on. All their stress and frustration in making this place look perfect worked because it looks like a dream, which is appropriate considering the theme of the night: Making Dreams Happen.

"Deep breaths," I whisper to myself as I walk around the dance floor, watching all the happy couples enjoying themselves. I keep walking, hoping to find Jake. Hoping to let my night begin. In the crowd, I finally find my knight in shining armor, wearing a traditional black tuxedo with a white shirt and black tie. His hair is the perfect balance of messy and put together. I can see his baby blue eyes even from this distance.

Smiling to myself, I start walking toward him. He sees me, and a carefree smile softens his features.

Butterflies are suddenly flapping wildly in my stomach, and I realize this is what dreams are made of. This is perfection. This is what the books talk about.

I may not be Cinderella, but tonight I'm starting to feel like I'm finally getting my very own happily ever after.

2

BUT UNLIKE YOU, I NEEDED TO FIND ME TO SURVIVE.

Dimah is an Arabic word meaning 'downpour'. I wish I was as strong as the name my mother gave me. I wish I was responsible for a downpour. Instead, I feel closer to light rain—almost inaudible, causing no change. Barely even noticeable.

Every morning, I wake up with the same utter lack of motivation. The same lack of desire to get changed and go to school. Instead, I wake up with the urge to escape, to run away—to hide. I can't do that though. I won't. I'm the only one here for my mom, and I don't know what she'd do without me.

I don't want to be a burden so I get up, hit the shower, brush my teeth, then stare at my open closet. Blue, pink, green, yellow—the colors of my clothes pop out, but I ignore them all. Instead, as usual, I opt for ripped black jeans, combat boots, and a black sweatshirt. A black beanie covers my brown hair. Running downstairs, I find my mother already gone to work.

On the table, there's a plate of eggs and toast next to a

sticky note that says, *Don't wait up for me today—18-hour shift. Love you, Dimah. – Mom.*

I finish my breakfast, get on my bike, and ride to school. Just three months until winter break; just nine until graduation. Then, I'll have a new start. A new place. Everything gets left behind and it'll be like high school never happened—like that day never happened.

I park my bike in the usual spot, take off my helmet, and hang it over the side. I look at the place I initially thought would change my life for the better, realizing again how wrong I was. Taking a deep breath, I walk with my head down, eyes on my feet, headphones in my ears. Music helps to drown out the memories coming back to me in flashes as I put one foot determinedly in front of the next. I enter the main hallway, eyes still downcast, and only look up when I notice I'm about to run into someone. Glancing up, I see it's the same guy who saw me outside yesterday—the same guy who almost saw me fall apart. My eyes linger longer than they should, enough time for him to give me a smile.

"Hey," he says.

I study him, wondering what's going through his mind, wondering what his sudden interest is in talking to me. He transferred here toward the end of last year, but not once has he said hello, not once has he given me the time of day—not even a smile. So why now?

"Whatever bet you've made, give it up," I answer, my voice low enough for only him to hear. I won't do this. I take the right side of the hall and walk away. When I feel eyes on me, I turn briefly to find him staring at me. I don't know what the deal is, but I'm sick of being the butt of the joke. I just wish people would let me fade into the shadows—where I belong.

"Hey, Dim, why you gotta be so mopey?" someone asks. Not surprisingly, they don't care to hear my response.

"I mean, just because the guy hit it and quit it doesn't mean you should be mad," another guy adds, the voices merging into the background noise.

"Man, she really changed over the summer," a girl from my biology class murmurs as I walk by. Ignoring her, I make my way toward my usual table in the cafeteria, the one closest to the trashcan—where no one sits but me. Being the outcast has never been better.

"She may be hiding under all that black, but she's still the same girl she was last year," adds another voice.

"Whore," one of Janice's minions' whispers.

Not the most unique insult I've heard in the last couple of months. Not even close to the worst, either.

"Seriously, unbelievable," Janice—fucking Janice—says from the popular table. My fingers twitch at my side, my hands desperate to get a piece of her. My body desperate to defend myself.

Dimah.

Downpour.

I wish I could draw from that strength and finally have the courage to stick up for myself.

Instead, I cower like always. With my head down and my tray in hand, I walk to my table and sit. I look at my calendar, counting down the days; counting down to the weekend. The break. The End.

Dreams Come True

"Hey, beautiful," Jacob says.

I swear I sigh audibly, admiring how handsome he is. "Hi," I respond shyly. His hand settles on the small of my back, and little shocks of electricity come over me in waves, leaving goosebumps all over my arms. I can't believe this is happening.

"You look amazing," he whispers in my ear.

"You look wonderful," I tell him honestly.

"Thank you for coming tonight."

"Thank you for inviting me. This is your senior prom after all. I didn't expect you to bring a junior with you."

I didn't expect him to want to bring me is what I want to say.

"You're not just a junior. You're my Dim," he says—and just like that, he's back to being the boy I grew up with. I remember how he coined the nickname—and how when other people said it, I felt like they were making fun of me, but when Jacob said it, it felt endearing.

He tucks a strand of hair behind my ear, his hand still at the small of my back as his lips come closer to mine. My pulse rises in response to his closeness, at the thought of his lips finally touching mine. I'm a little disappointed when those full lips move away, but the tingles are restored when they come close beside my ear. "Want to get out of here?" he whispers.

"We just got here." Well, at least I just got here. Maybe he's been here for a bit.

"I know, but I can think of a place where we could have more fun," he answers. I know I should say no. I should stay

here, where I told my mother I'd be. I'm not naïve. I know what a senior prom means.

"You think?" He smiles down at me—and all reason leaves my body, replaced by the thought of going somewhere with this handsome man, having his lips on mine.

"For sure," he says, grabbing my hands. He starts to walk, pulling me with him. I look behind me, taking in the beautiful décor, the dancing, the laughter. I wish we could stay for a little longer.

But then I look forward, see Jacob promising me the world with his smile, and my desire to stay fades away.

3

UNLIKE YOU, LOSING THE PALM OF MY HANDS TO THE
BRIGHTNESS OF THE SUN MEANT THE EARTH STOPPED
ROTATING AROUND MY THIGHS.

The final bell rings, marking the end of another mostly uneventful day. As I walk the halls, there's the same old name calling—the same I hear every day. Today was different in one way, though. It was worse.

I actually got insulted to my face instead of just behind my back. I got verbally torn down and ripped to pieces. I tried to mask how much that hurt me.

I think I failed.

"You should start standing up for yourself," a voice says, startling me as I put my books back into my locker, keeping out the ones I need to take home.

"You should mind your own business," I retort.

"It's funny how you can yell at me for no reason at all, but you can't tell other people to leave you alone," he answers.

I shut my locker. "Most other people just say things about me behind my back. You're the one that keeps hounding me face to face." I lengthen my stride, heading towards the exit.

"I wouldn't call it hounding," he calls out after me. "I'm just tired of seeing you like this."

My steps falter and I turn to face him—the guy who's calling me on my shit. "Tired of seeing me like what? Do you even know who I am?"

"Dimah Emerson. Senior. Motorcycle riding, black attire wearing, Taylor Swift listening."

"How would you even know—"

"That you listen to Taylor Swift?" he says, raising his brows in challenge.

I make a disgusted noise at the back of my throat and turn back to the door, but his hand shoots out, holding me in place. I look up at him; he looks down at me, waiting. "Yes," I sigh, rolling my eyes.

"You sure do crank it up; I can hear it through your headphones every morning when you park your bike next to my car."

"That's not—"

"It's true. You just can't tell because you're always walking with your head down. You may not know me, but I definitely know a little about you."

"Aron Lincoln." I counter. Glaring. "Football quarterback. Great grades. Girls want to be with you, guys want to be friends with you."

"So you know about me too, then," he says with a smirk.

"Enough to know I don't want to be talking to you. And I sure as hell don't need your advice," Pulling my arm out of his hold, I shove my way out the door and make my way toward my bike. Why does he even care? I know the answer: he doesn't. No one does.

And if it's too good to be true, it usually isn't true.

I wish I'd learned that a while back.

First Kiss

"So, where are we going?" I ask, full of curiosity as we step outside to face the cool of the night. It's May, so at least the cold doesn't bite—it just washes over us in a pleasant breeze.

"Right now, we're going to the car," he says, totally at ease.

I cling to his every word. Jacob. Jake Hastings. "Okay." That's all I can say anyway—I'm just a lovesick puppy following the lead of the guy whose attention I've been craving since the moment it was first gone. The boy who makes my heart beat so erratically. We drive in silence while I watch him from the passenger seat. The traffic lights we pass reflect on the glass, and the further we get from the school, the more eager I become.

Finally, the car comes to a stop at a hotel on the edge of town. Jake gets out, jogging around to open the passenger door for me. I blush, pleased; he definitely knows how to treat a woman. He was raised right, and I'm glad he hasn't changed much. Despite the years that have passed, despite how much time we were apart, he's still the same.

"Sorry I couldn't get a better place for us," he says sheepishly, gesturing toward the building.

"It's okay. This is perfect," I assure him. *The fact that he's tried to make this special is enough for me.*

"You deserve better," he says, stepping closer.

My back hits the car door. My breath hitches. Then, Jake places a soft, sweet kiss on my cheek, and I'm immediately lost in the swarm of feelings. My first kiss—with my first crush. I don't know how many people can say that.

"Thank you," I answer stupidly after he pulls away.

"Don't thank me just yet," he tells me. *A smile overtakes his face as he intertwines our fingers and pulls me in the direction of the hotel's entrance. We walk into the lobby, where I take a step back, waiting for him to head over to the counter.* *"We're good. I have the keys; I came to set this up earlier,"* he says.

My heart swells. He planned this earlier, for us. He was thinking about me. This wasn't just spur of the moment. I imagine walking into a hotel room with roses, candles, romantic music playing...

Just like a fairy tale.

4

LOSING ME, FOR ME MEANT THE STARS STOPPED SHINING
LIFE INTO THE DARKNESS OF MY SKIN.

Locker room talk is a little different in the girls' locker room. It's a little more targeted, a little crueler. Not to everyone though. Just to me. But it's the last class I have today, so I'll suck it up. I change into my gym clothes and leave the venomous locker room.

I sit on the bleachers, waiting for the teachers to give instructions. Waiting to get this day over with.

"Okay, today we're playing dodgeball. I still can't believe some schools have banned this beautiful sport," Mr. Walker says.

"Come down and let's stretch," the other teacher, Ms. Tillman, adds. I leave my seat on the bleachers and take a spot on the floor, far enough away from everyone else to have my own space. Ms. Tillman takes us through a few stretches before ordering everyone to do ten pushups. I'm on the ninth when the gym door opens and the room starts to buzz; I finish the set and then sit up to find Aron Lincoln talking to the teachers. Of course, the entire class is practically vibrating with anticipation— his mere presence has them all staring. I go back to stretching, working first my legs, and then my arms while Ms. Tillman and Mr. Walker talk to Aron.

"Okay class, Mr. Lincoln will be joining us this semester," Mr. Walker says out loud.

Surprisingly, everyone cheers and claps in response— they *literally* clap for him.

"You've got to be fucking kidding," I mutter to myself.
"Get up and head to the wall," Ms. Tillman states. "We're going to split you into two teams." We all obey, walking toward the walls at different speeds.

I reach the wall, making sure I'm separated from everyone else. It's not like they mind being far away from me, anyway. As I cross my arms and wait for the unavoidable number system, Ms. Tillman begins to speak, "Actually, we're going to have two captains today. So Janice and Aron, each of you will head a team. Let's get started."

I lean my head back against the wall, waiting for the inevitable to happen.

Janice goes first, choosing one of the guys from the football team. Big surprise there—I'm sure if it weren't for Aron being the other captain, she would've picked him instead. I wait for Aron to choose, disinterested in the process and ready to get this class over with.

"Emerson," Aron says, pointing at me. I swear people gasp—seriously fucking gasp—at the mention of my name. I'm too stunned to move, so I just stand there staring, waiting to see if he made a mistake. He only smiles, so I begin to walk slowly toward him, my steps cautious. Being picked last usually meant no one would even

Not the End

notice me at all, but being picked first—especially by him—gives the student body too much to think about.

Why would he pick the pathetic gothic girl, the laughingstock of the school? Doesn't he know any better?

The smile still hasn't left his face, even as Janice chooses the next person for her team. As Aron takes his turn, his gaze stays on me until I'm standing behind him, hiding behind his wide frame. I don't know what his plan is; I don't know what his intentions are, but they can't be good. They never are.

Once the teams are chosen, we make our way to opposite sides of the gym, watching the teachers line the middle of the court with dodgeballs.

Dodgeball. It's so therapeutic. It's the one time I can channel all my anger into throwing things at people I don't like—people that don't like me. It's one of the only sports I excel at, probably because it gives me an outlet. The whistle blows and the game begins. I grab a red ball that rolls toward me, and with all my strength, I toss it over to the other side, eliminating one of Janice's minions with a hit to the leg.

I jump, dodge, turn, and avoid balls being thrown at me. The game continues until there are three players on my side of the court, and four on the other side. From the corner of my eye, I see Aron take a ball and toss it straight into the stomach of one of the players, sending him out of the game. Soon it's just Aron and I on our side, and Janice and Everett— another asshole—on the other.

Balls immediately start to fly from one side of the court to the other as people scream encouragement. I grab one of the balls; Aron grabs another. We both throw them at the same time, hitting our targets on the other side. His ball ends up hitting Everett mid jump, causing him to trip. My ball hurtles through the air, hitting Janice in the face. She screams.

"That bitch did that on purpose!" she yells, running toward Ms. Tillman.

"Yes, she did!" one of her minions yells.

"I thought hitting someone in the face wasn't allowed!" Janice adds

How much could it have hurt anyway? Suck it up.

"It's not," Mr. Walker's voice booms. "Ms. Emerson, did you do that on purpose?" he asks. I'm about to answer when I feel Aron at my side.

"She didn't." Two words. That's all it takes, and Mr. Walker nods in response.

"We don't have a winning team yet. Janice, you can go back on the court against Aron. Dimah, you're out of the game. Let's see which team wins," Mr. Walker says. I hate that he's punishing me anyway. It was a mistake—not one that I regret—but a mistake nonetheless.

"She can have the win," Aron says, still standing next to me.

"We can just repeat the point." Janice's tone has changed from whining to flirtatious. I'm sure everyone in the gym can tell.

"Let's do it again," Mr. Walker instructs. "Keep it fair." I walk over to the bleachers, watching as Janice takes her position opposite Aron. The whistle echoes around the room; Janice runs to grab a ball, but Aron stays in place. She throws an air ball he could easily have caught, but he puts his palm out to let the ball hit him.

"Janice's team wins," Ms. Tillman declares. Half of the students erupt in applause, while the other half are clearly confused as to what happened. I don't take time to question it; I just walk into the locker room.

Alone in the shower, I run the water hot, eager to wash away the sweat from the day. It's going to be one of those days where I wait for everyone else to leave, I can tell. I shampoo my hair, taking as long as possible. Who cares if I end up leaving twenty minutes after the bell? I'd rather avoid the drama anyway.

Hotel Room

IT'S DEFINITELY NOT LIKE I PICTURED IT. WHEN WE WALK *into the room, there aren't any candles.*

No romantic music, no flower petals on the bed.

It's just a room. Just a bed.

Just the regular lighting—not at all how I envisioned my first time.

But when I look at the guy closing the door, I realize I don't care about the perfect fairytale as long as I have my prince. "Hey," *he says, taking measured steps towards me.*

"Hi," *I reply.*

"I've been waiting for this for a long time," *he says, his eyes predatory.*

"Me too." *And I have. Years, actually. That's how long I've waited for a first kiss. He closes the distance quickly and his lips collide with my own. But this kiss is not like the one he gave me earlier—this one is more controlling, more desperate. Almost harsh.*

"*Wait,*" *I tell him.* "*We're moving too fast.*"

"*Wait for what?*" *he asks, his hand going to my back, lowering the zipper on my gown.*

"*Shouldn't we take this slow?*" *I ask.*

"*Seriously? You've been wanting this for forever and now you want to take it slow?*" *he asks, obviously frustrated.*

I pause, considering his words. "*You're right,*" *I whisper. I can't back out now. I did come into this hotel room with him, after all.*

Pulling me towards him, he says, "*Come here.*"

"Where are you going?" I ask, after he finishes. I pull *the sheets closer, shielding my body from his eyes.*

"*You think I'm staying here?*" *he spits back, his tone so unlike the Jacob I thought I knew—nothing at all like the Jacob that asked me to go to prom with him.*

I feel like my heart has been pulled from my chest and torn to pieces—like my dress. "*You're not?*"

"*No,*" *he says coldly. Then he leaves the room.*

5

LOSING THE GOODNESS MY MAMA POURED INTO MY HEART
AS SHE GAVE LIFE TO ME.

I get out of the shower when I realize everyone has left. I take hold of my towel and walk to the changing area, where the lockers are—and find my gym locker already open. I get closer to it and see that although my book bag is still there, my clothes are gone. I run back to the shower. My gym clothes are gone, too.

Fuck. Seriously?

I should know better by now. I mean, I did hit her in the face with a ball.

I hit the girl that's made making fun of me her new obsession. I should've expected retaliation.

Although, really, it isn't *getting back* at me at all. It's more like just continuing to harass me—and honestly, I don't think a million balls to the face would even come close to putting us on equal ground.

What do I do? I have no clothes in my gym locker, and even my dirty gym clothes are gone. My phone is still an option, though; I could call mom and have her pick me up—but how do I explain the sudden absence of my clothing? How do I explain to her the hell I've been living in for the last few months? I shouldn't make her worry about something she has no control over.

I look around, searching for anything I could use to cover myself, because I'm literally wearing a towel right now. Thankfully I still have a way to get home—my motorcycle—but a towel is definitely not going to cut it.

Wait—my school locker! Maybe I have a sweater or something in there? I remember leaving clothes in there before; I'll just run over to my locker and check.

If Ms. Tillman was still here, she'd likely be able to find something in the lost and found for me to wear, but as usual, she's gone as soon as the majority of the girls leave the locker room. She knows I like to linger, and while I usually like that she gives me the space, I seriously wish she hadn't given me space today.

I tip-toe out of the locker room and start walking toward the door leading to the hallway.

"I guess this gym class operates a little differently."

I freeze mid-step. *Fuck. Aron's still here?* Clutching my towel a little more tightly, I turn to face him. "Why are you still here?" I ask, resigned to the fact that I'm standing in the middle of the gym with nothing but a towel wrapped around me.

"I wanted to make sure you were okay," he says—like he truly cares about my wellbeing.

"Why would you think I wasn't going to be?" I ask warily. *Did he have something to do with this?*

"I hear what they say about you," he starts.

I turn around to walk away from him. I don't need a

recap of what's said about me, what people think about me...what *he* probably thinks about me.

"Well, you did hit her in the face with a ball, so I figured she'd try to get back at you somehow. I just wanted to make sure you were okay," he says.

I swear, I almost believe him. "Why do you care all of a sudden?" Might as well put it out there, since that's really what I'm thinking.

He takes in a deep breath and blows it out. "Because what they're doing isn't right. What you *let them do* isn't right..."

"What I *let them do* to me?" I spit back. "Do you think I let them take all my clothes so I have to figure out what to wear to go home? Do you think I wanted that?" The nerve of him to believe that this is my choice, that I've ever wanted *any* of this!

"Yes," he says with absolute certainty. When I scoff, he presses on. "You let them because you don't stand up for yourself to stop it."

"I can't do this right now. I won't." I turn away and walk out the door.

Aron jogs after me. "You shouldn't be out here like this."

"I don't exactly have much of a choice," I tell him. "Just go back to the locker room. Look, I have a shirt and some pants I can give you."

I want to say no—to reject his offer—but walking around the school in just a towel is not the best option. "Thanks," I mutter, turning to walk back into the locker room.

A minute later, Aron comes in with sweatpants and a

jersey—his jersey. He hands them over to me. "Here. I'll wait outside," he says, letting himself out.

I don't give myself an opportunity to question his motives. Instead, I walk into the changing rooms and throw on his sweatpants, rolling the waist over a few times so they don't slide off my hips. It's crazy that they make me feel so small. Then I take hold of the jersey—with number twenty-one displayed on the back, just below his last name. Lincoln.

Most girls in this school would die to wear a guy's jersey, but not me. I'm just glad I don't have to walk around nude.

My shoes are gone too—of course. I guess when they do something, they do it right. I'm surprised they left my book bag; I guess books probably aren't as important to them. They're important to me, though.

I hang my towel inside my locker. Locking it this time, I throw my bag over my shoulder and walk out. Aron's sitting on the bleachers, looking down at his phone. I cough to get his attention. I still find it odd that he would wait to make sure I was okay—but while I'm definitely skeptical, I'm also grateful for his help.

"Sorry," he says, putting his phone in his pocket. "I didn't notice you were out."

I wiggle my toes. "No shoes, no noise."

"They're rotten people," he says, exasperated.

"I guess."

"They're bullies. I can't believe the shit they get away with." He says this like he doesn't get away with much. "Like you don't get away with a lot because you're a football player? Cheerleaders are pretty much cut from the exact same cloth." Well, maybe not the same, but similar.

"I wouldn't dare do something so cruel."

"You're saying you never played a joke on a friend by hiding his clothes?"

"They aren't playing a prank on you and they aren't your friends," he replies, and I wonder how much he knows. How much people have told him—and how much of it is the actual truth.

"I'll take that as a yes," I state, ignoring the painful truth in his comments—I already know they aren't my friends and this isn't a prank. There's no point in preaching to the choir.

"Maybe one time," he says with a carefree smile. "But we made sure he had clothes by the time he left."

"Thanks again for these," I tell him, pulling at his shirt.

"Any time. It looks good on you, Emerson," he says, and I can't help but chuckle.

"Yeah, right. Anyway, I should go."

"You ride a bike," he tells me.

I watch him, trying to figure out what point he's trying to make. He's already told me he knows I ride a bike. He's seen me ride it before, and I apparently park next to him every day. "Yes," I reply.

"I mean, you can't ride your bike without shoes."

Crap. That's probably not the safest idea, but what other choice is there? "I'll deal."

"You don't have to. I can give you a ride home," he says, following me toward the exit.

"I'm okay, really. You've done enough." I don't know where all this kindness is coming from, but I don't trust it.

"I don't mind."

"I can ride barefoot."

"That's not the safest thing to do," he chastises gently. "Let me give you a ride. I promise I won't try anything," he says, followed by a small laugh. I know he's joking, but I can't get myself to laugh back. Not at this.

"I'm good." We finally reach the doors and exit the school. The parking lot is deserted—with the exceptions of a few cars in the teacher's parking lot, his car, and my bike. There aren't any after school programs on Thursdays. No club meetings, no practices.

"I'm sorry if that came off weird," he says suddenly. "I don't mean to creep you out. I just don't think it's safe for you to go barefoot. Please, let me give you a ride. If it makes you feel safer, you can drive."

I can see in his eyes that he's being genuine—but then again, I stopped trusting in my ability to perceive things accurately a long time ago. "You're going to let me drive?" I ask. He doesn't even know me, not well anyway. Yet here he is, waiting for me to tell him whether I can drive myself home in his car. Part of me wishes I could just accept his kindness and take it just as that, but another part of me knows better.

"If that makes you feel more at ease, yes, you can drive. I can even sit in the back and you can pretend to be my driver," he says with an easy-going smile.

We reach our parking spots. "Okay," I finally give in.

"Okay," he says, handing me the keys to his Wrangler.

"You must be really trusting to let me drive your car. How do you even know I can drive?"

"You ride a bike. I'm praying you learned to drive a car, too. Still, I'm willing to take the risk," he says, opening the door to the driver's side. It makes me sad to realize that the gesture doesn't have the same effect on me as it used to. I take hold of the door and let myself in, closing it immediately after. He runs over to the passenger side.

"So, you want me to sit in the back or the front?"

"You were serious about that whole thing?"

"Yep, whatever makes you most comfortable."

"Front is okay," I say. I'm driving, so technically, I'm still in control.

"You sure?"

"Yup," I reply. He gets in and puts on his seatbelt. I start the car, put it in reverse, and begin backing out of the parking spot.

We drive in silence for a few minutes before Aron speaks again. "So, do you smoke often?"

I can't believe this is the question he decides to ask now. I give him a side-long look. "Not really. Just that day."

"A one-time thing?"

"Yeah."

"Bad day?" he asks. I can hear the concern in his voice —a concern I don't quite comprehend.

"Something like that," I tell him. Actually, it's more like my mother expected me to be at homecoming and I showed up thinking I could do it, thinking that the past was the past and I could let it go. But the moment I walked into the room, the wolves found their prey and came after me. The whispers continued, and I was once again the laughingstock of the room. Just like before—just like always. I couldn't stand there. I couldn't be there anymore.

"You use drugs as a way to cope?"

"I guess so."

"That's not a good idea. That's how addictions start, and they don't really help."

"You sound like someone with first-hand experience."

"Something like that," he says, echoing my earlier words.

"I thought you said you don't smoke."

"I don't. Not anymore. You shouldn't either."

"No need to worry. It's not like I'm going to ever do it again." No way in hell. It made me feel disoriented and lost, like I had no control of myself. Dizzy and desperate, and I actually felt all the pressure and anxiety I usually push down so deeply. I never want to experience that again.

"Good," he says, watching me.

"Are you always this nice to people?" I ask, eager to know if there are still good people out there.

"Only to those that deserve it." For some reason, I feel like there's something hidden deep within him, a thread that wants to connect us; it doesn't matter, because I refuse to let it. "Can I play some music?" he asks sheepishly.

"It's your car," I remind him.

"Right," he says, messing with the radio.

I take another turn, getting closer and closer to home

— to my safe haven. Suddenly, Taylor Swift starts playing loudly. I burst out laughing.

"I thought you'd enjoy that," he says with a chuckle.

"Wasn't expecting it to be on your instant playlist."

"I told you I could hear it playing from your headphones. I was intrigued."

"So intrigued that you downloaded the songs and kept them on your queue?"

"What can I say? When something intrigues me, I get invested."

We've heard most of the songs from Taylor's latest album by the time I pull onto my street and park in front of my house. "Thank you again. For everything."

"You don't have to thank me. Just..." He pauses, then sighs, "Just think about finally standing up for yourself," he finishes.

"I'll think about it," I respond, unbuckling my seatbelt and opening the door. I walk around the front of the car and Aron meets me there.

"I just realized something," he says.

A deeply-rooted fear springs to the surface of my mind. "What?"

"You left your bike at the school."

"Yes," I state slowly.

"It means you don't have a way to get to school tomorrow."

Shit. That's true. "I'll take the bus," I tell him. I haven't done that in a while—because taking the bus is subjecting myself to further harassment—but I can suck it up for one day.

"Nonsense. I'll pick you up."

"I'm sure you have better things to do," I tell him.

"At 7:30 in the morning? Nope. Nothing better. I don't live too far from here either, actually. I can be outside your door at 7:35."

"You don't have to."

"I know. I don't have to do anything. But I will. So I'll see you tomorrow, bright and early," he says with a smile as he walks the rest of the way to the door of his car.

I step onto the sidewalk; he gets in and waves goodbye. As I watch the car retreat, I try to figure out what to make of this—what to make of him.

6

BUT FOR YOU, LOSING ME WAS LIKE DRINKING TEA
WITHOUT HONEY.

At 7am sharp, my alarm rings. I toss and turn in the bed, unwilling to get up. Last night, I barely got any sleep; I spent the night with my thoughts lost somewhere between the past and the present. I thought about what I've been through—and what's changed. I also spent more time than I'd care to admit thinking about Aron Lincoln.

I can't figure him out—or the game he's playing. The alarm rings again, reminding me it's time to face the music once more. Getting up, I push myself through my normal routine, getting ready for class, before running downstairs to pull Aron's sweatpants and jersey out of the dryer.

I head to the kitchen to find my mom sitting at the breakfast table. "Hi, dear," she says with a tired smile.

"Hi, Mom."

"Here, sit down and have some breakfast," she says, getting up from her chair to hand me a glass of orange juice, simultaneously setting a plate of pancakes in front of me.

"Thank you. Have you gotten any sleep yet?" I ask just to keep the conversation going; I already know what the answer is.

"I haven't yet, but I will in a few minutes. I just wanted to see you. I feel like I don't see you as often anymore," she tells me, her hands cradling my face.

She's right. We don't see each other much since she works such crazy shifts. It's fitting though, since I feel like I don't see myself as often either—just glimpses of me every now and then. I take a bite of pancake. "I've missed you too, Mom."

"I love you, Dimah."

"I know. I love you, too."

I finish my breakfast, placing her plate and mine together in the dishwasher. The moment I close the dishwasher door, I hear a horn honking outside. "Oh, that's me," I say, a little too eagerly.

"Someone's picking you up?" my mom asks, intrigued. She may not know exactly what happened to me last year, but she definitely knows something changed. She probably thinks it's just normal teenage crap though; I've seen books on her nightstand about the nightmare years of raising teens. Maybe she thinks I'm just going through the process and that it's all normal. I bet she's hoping it'll end soon. She's never questioned my newfound obsession with the color black, my lack of friends, or my sudden lack of enthusiasm for school. Still, she understands me enough not to push or pry.

Mom didn't even blink when I came back from

grandma Elle's looking like a completely different person–didn't bat an eyelid when I asked her to get me a motorcycle instead of the car she'd planned on buying me. But just because she allowed it doesn't mean she didn't tell me about all the dangers of riding one. She even had me spend time taking lessons.

"Yeah, I had to leave my bike at the school yesterday."

"How come?" she asks.

"I ran out of gas," I lie. That's a much better, much faster explanation than telling her someone stole my clothes and shoes.

"Is this a new friend?" she asks, obviously curious to see if I've allowed more people into my life.

"Just someone from school being helpful," I tell her. "Anyway, I've gotta go," I add before she has a chance to ask me anything else. I run out the door to find the same Wrangler I got the chance to drive yesterday waiting for me outside. As I close the distance, Aron steps from the driver's side and walks around to the passenger door.

"Good morning," he says, with a too-bright smile.

"Morning," I mumble. He begins to open the passenger door, but as I start walking toward it, he gets in and shuts the door. I stop, staring at him. *What the hell is going on?*

He rolls down the window. "We're going to be late for school. Are you driving or what?"

I smile and walk to the driver's side; when I get in, Taylor Swift is already playing. Laughing at how odd this feels, I shift the car to drive, easing into the strange yet comforting peace Aron seems to bring.

"See, this is nice," he says after the second song on the album ends.

I keep my eyes on the road. "What's nice?"

"This. I feel like I have a personal chauffeur."

"Don't get used to it. I'm back on my bike today. Two wheels are better than four."

"Not when it rains."

"That, I cannot argue with."

"Also, not when you're barefoot," he adds.

"Thank you for the reminder."

"Maybe next time, *you* give *me* a ride to school. I'm dying to see how you handle that bike."

"Maybe." I say the word out loud, but it takes a second for me to realize it.

He smiles and nods as the third song begins to play, and all it takes is a few more songs before we reach the parking lot. I park the Jeep right where it usually goes—next to my bike. I open the door, letting myself out of the car, and when I look up, I realize all eyes are on us.

I guess I should've seen that coming. I wait for the other shoe to drop, for someone to laugh at me and tell me how pathetic I am once again. When they do, will Aron give me the same disgusted look everyone else does as he walks away?

I'm waiting for Janice. But nothing happens.

"I'll see you later?" Aron asks, a little unsure.

"Maybe," I respond, retreating from the searching eyes—eyes that are wondering why a pathetic gothic chick like me is driving the quarterback's car. I head inside as quickly as I can, my gaze locked on the floor as if it holds the secrets to all the world's greatest mysteries.

Not the End

I make it all the way to my locker to exchange some of the books before I realize Aron's jersey and sweatpants are still in my bag. I guess I can return them at the end of gym class, considering he's now one of our permanent students.

Walking to class, I hear the usual name-calling. And I feel the usual way. Like I'm the dirt under their shoes.

"What the fuck is she doing with him?" Janice says loudly as I enter homeroom.

The Monday After

IT WAS MONDAY. I HADN'T HEARD ANYTHING FROM JACOB THE *entire weekend. I got a cab home on Friday, but I didn't leave the hotel room right away. Part of me was hoping he'd come back, that he'd change his mind and realize he didn't want to leave me by myself. I was hoping he'd go back to the sweet guy he was years ago.*

That wasn't the case.

He didn't return.

And after two hours of crying, I decided it was time to go home. I didn't want my mom worrying about me.

I stayed home all weekend, the volume on my phone's ringer set as loud as it would go. I waited for him to reach out to me, to call me, check up on me. Saturday passed by with no contact.

Why did he leave so quickly after? Maybe an emergency?

Maybe he felt enclosed and claustrophobic in the room. Maybe there was a reason he couldn't stay.

That's what I told myself for the entire weekend.

On Sunday, my mom asked me if I had any photos of the two of us; I told her no.

She asked me if I had fun at prom; I told her yes.

As the day went on without a word, I looked him up on social media and found that he'd spent the weekend partying with friends; there were photos of some girls from school surrounding him—girls from the popular crowd.

Maybe he didn't tell me because he knew I wouldn't fit in with them. Maybe he didn't want me to be bored. Maybe he wanted me all to himself. Or at least, that's what I kept telling myself as the doubt began to creep in.

Monday morning, I take the bus to school just like I do every day. But something is different this time.

I'm different, yes—but there's something else, too. Whispers and quiet conversations start and stop as I make my way to the back of the bus. For a second it feels like they're talking about me, laughing at something to do with me...but that can't be the case.

I shake it off as paranoia.

When I walk out of the bus, I hear more whispers.

"Did you hear about what happened this weekend?"

"With that slut, Dimah?"

I'm about to stop and say something when I realize I must have heard it wrong. They must be talking about someone else. I grab my bag, walk out of the bus, and head inside. I have first period with Jacob, so I quickly swap out my books and head to homeroom.

Not the End

The whispers continue. It feels like I'm in an episode of the Twilight Zone.

I make it through the fifteen minutes of homeroom and head straight to first period; I take my usual seat and wait for the class to fill up. Right on time, Jacob—as tall and handsome as ever—makes his appearance. I sit a little higher in my chair, waiting for his eyes to find me. He doesn't even look at me; instead, he walks to the back of the classroom, taking his usual seat.

Maybe he didn't notice me. Maybe he had a tough weekend. Maybe he's struggling with something?

I hope his family's okay.

Class begins. I tamp down my insecurities and try to reassure myself that it's all going to be okay. When the end-of-class bell rings, I put my things in my bag—and see Jacob walk past and out the door from the corner of my eye. I follow him, ready to talk about this weekend.

About us. About what's next.

Outside the classroom, I stop in my tracks. I recognize Jacob's back; I also recognize the girl he's with by her auburn hair. I stare at them, making out right in the middle of the hall, in the middle of everyone. People watch the spectacle as he pulls her closer. She runs her fingers through his hair—and as much as I want to, I can't look away.

"Jacob." His name leaves my mouth in a whisper I doubt he'll hear. The students start hollering, cheering them on. Finally, they break the kiss.

"Jacob has completed his challenge!" Janice announces. I have no idea what challenge she's talking about. Maybe kissing her in the middle of the hall is the challenge.

Maybe he didn't want to kiss her, I tell myself.

Because I'm still telling myself that he wants me.

"What challenge?" *I ask, finally finding my voice. All eyes turn to me—including Jacob's—and people begin chattering. More whispers. More comments I can't hear.*

More feeling like they're talking about me.

"Oh, you haven't heard about the challenge, dear?" *Janice purrs. I've never liked her. She's poisonous, mean, evil. She hurts people and doesn't care.*

"What challenge?" *I ask again. My eyes search Jacob's, waiting for something—waiting for him to explain everything to me.*

"He deflowered a virgin," *Janice says, looking me straight in the eyes.*

7

EASY TO REPLACE WITH SUGAR.

I don't know when I stopped letting the comments in the hall get to me, but I think that's one of the better choices I've made in the last few months. That, along with spending the summer as far away from here as I could get.

My regular classes end, and the only thing left is gym. Instead of changing in the locker room like I'd normally do, I walk into the bathroom during the break and change into my gym clothes.

The lengths one has to go to in order to avoid conflict around here are outrageous.

I walk into the locker room to put my bag away just as people are leaving. Once again, I feel the tension in the air. Some of the girls, especially Janice's minions, stare at me disdainfully before going back to whatever conversation they were having—probably about me. I wish it wasn't. I wish last year could be buried deep down, but somehow people still haven't gotten over it.

Easy.

Slut.

Virgin.

Bet.

I walk into the gym just as class is about to start. "Today we're playing volleyball," Mr. Walker states, his voice quickly silencing the room. "We're going to stretch, then each of you will need to find a partner so you can practice bumps, sets, and spikes. Then we'll play a game." Some students cheer, and I feel a smile creep onto my lips.

Ms. Tillman guides us in the stretches and as soon as we're done, everyone looks for a partner. I don't move, but some of the cheerleaders head straight to the few football players in our class. And Janice? Well of course, she heads straight toward Aron—and I watch their interaction from my place on the floor.

"I'm good."

I hear those words come out of Aron's mouth, and I watch in shock as he walks away from Janice. I don't think I'm the only one who heard it, either; silence overtakes the room again. Janice stares daggers at the back of his head. Every step he takes away from her only makes her angrier.

I look down at my feet, at the small scar I got when I was learning how to ride this summer. Accidentally burned it on the muffler—a perpetual reminder of change.

"Want to practice together?" At the sound of his voice, I jerk my head up, only to find him looking down at *me*.

"Um…" I'm a little stumped. Yesterday, he picked me

first for dodgeball, and today he turned down Janice to choose me?

"I'll take that as a yes," he says, extending his hand.

I slip my palm into his and he pulls me up from the floor. "I don't get you," I utter.

"What don't you get?"

"The most popular girl in this whole school just asked you to be her partner and you turned her down. Then you ask me. Why?" *It's a new year. He's a senior. Graduation is coming.* I don't want to be this year's challenge. Those are the only thoughts in my mind as I ask him to be honest with me.

"Do I really need a reason? I just didn't want to be partnered up with her," he answers, not clearing anything up for me.

I don't know why I expected him to. "But you want to be partnered up with me? That's what I don't understand."

"Why's it so hard for you to understand someone wants you?" he asks, and while I know he's talking about choosing me as his volleyball partner, I can't help but think about what else he could mean. No one would want me—and if they do, it's because they don't have another choice.

"Before the homecoming dance, you never said a word to me."

"I was a different person then."

"Really? How so?"

"Give me a ride on your motorcycle and maybe I'll tell you," he says with a wink.

Is he flirting with me? God, why is my mind so messed up? Why am I damaged? "Hmph."

"Playing hard to get," he says.

I shoot even bigger daggers at him than Janice did earlier. "Despite what you may have heard, I am not easy," I tell him, turning to walk away. I reach the bin of volleyballs, but stop when I feel Aron closing in.

From behind me, he says, "That's not what I meant to imply."

"That's what it sounded like."

"I'm an idiot. Sometimes shit comes out of my mouth that maybe shouldn't. And yeah, I've heard a lot about you," he says.

He's said that before, but this time it's like someone punched me in the stomach; all the contents suddenly want desperately to spill out at my feet. "Of course you have," I whisper, my anger rising. Despite the rage, I keep my voice low. "And that's why you thought you'd befriend me—because you think I'm a slut. You thought you found yourself an easy lay. So is there some bet happening again this year? Another challenge? A rite of passage? Because I'm not a virgin anymore, if that's the case."

"No. That's not it at all. I know the rumors are lies; I know you're not an easy lay. You just fell for the wrong person. And he was an asshole if he didn't see how smart and beautiful and strong you are..." When I roll my eyes, he adds, "You *are* stronger than you think—stronger than you show."

My voice is still low as I mutter defiantly, "You don't know me."

"Not as much as I want to, but I'm trying."

Not the End

"Stop trying," I tell him. We walk back to take our position at one of the nets set up around the gym. I may not want to continue having this conversation, but I do have to follow directions.

"I'm not going to stop—not until you give me a good reason for why I should," he says, bumping the ball over to me.

I have a lot of reasons why he should back off, reasons not to trust him. Reasons not to trust anyone...

But I'm also tired of pushing people away.

Conflicted, I shake my head. "I don't get it."

He smiles patiently. "Not all things are meant to be understood."

Rites of Passage

"*I*T'S A TRADITION FOR THE GRADUATING PLAYERS TO DO A FEW *tasks in order to successfully pass the mantle. They all pick a card from a jar which gives them a mission. They range from basic challenges like TP'ing someone's house to more challenging tasks like deflowering a virgin. Jacob here got the short end of the stick and selected the virgin card," Janice explains— like it's a game, like it doesn't affect people. Like it isn't affecting me. I stand in the hallway, helpless as everyone watches Janice, Jacob and me.*

"You thought it was going to be impossible, right babe?" she asks, running her fingers up his chest.

His eyes are heartbreakingly full of amusement. "Yeah," *he says casually.*

"I told him he should pretend we'd broken up, and then invite Ms. Emerson to prom. She's had a crush on him for years now," Janice sneers, enjoying her moment.

She's making a performance of humiliating me; she's talking to everyone else, pushing in the knife. I feel a panic attack creeping in. I'm ready to lose it all and just cry. Or scream...

Or fight.

"I mean, it definitely sucked not going to prom with my boyfriend, but after he handled his disgusting task, he came right back to me—and with enough time for us to have the last dance, too" she continues.

Serpent.

"She really thought you cared about her," Janice adds, chuckling as she looks up at Jacob.

He pulls her closer to his side. "Not even a little."

With those four words, he breaks the fragile hold I'm keeping on my emotions. The tears start to fall; I want to run, but I'm frozen in place.

"Easy lay though. One night—that's all it took," Janice says. Stretching up on her toes, she kisses Jake before continuing her demoralizing little performance. "I mean, thinking about him with her was vomit inducing, but we just had to do it. Plus, he said it was so anticlimactic he couldn't wait to leave anyway." Janice shrugs as everyone laughs out loud, having a wonderful time at my expense. Then she sighs dramatically, flipping a hand in my direction. "Such an easy flower to pluck. I still can't believe she gave it up like that—he barely even had to make an effort, even though it's unbelievable to think she

thought Jacob would leave me for her. Why would he leave me for such a fat, plain, slutty bitch?"

I can't hear anything anymore. I feel like a fish out of water, drowning. With tears streaming down my face, I walk away, but the chants still surround me. People are cheering for Janice and Jacob, calling me all sorts of names.

Slut.

Whore.

Easy.

Desperate.

Fat.

Ugly.

Over and over again, I hear their mocking. The door closes behind me; it's raining outside but I don't care.

I run home as the rain pours. When I get to my house, I run into my room and hide under the blankets—but the voices just scream louder, echoing in my mind, demeaning me.

But what I hear, louder than any voice from the crowd, is his silence.

He never cared about me.

8

THOUGH WE BOTH KNOW I TASTE PURELY SWEET LIKE SUGARCANE.

"You should stay away from Aron," a very familiar voice says from behind me. It's a voice I've come to hate, one that still causes me to jump every time I hear it.

Janice's voice. I can't believe the power she has over me.

"I'm talking to you, slut," she says—louder this time.

I flinch again. Dropping my books, I turn to face her, but she pushes me against the locker, drawing the attention of other students who turn to watch. Sharks who've smelled the blood in the water and are eager to see the attack.

"I—"

"You what?" Janice snarls.

"I don't understand."

"Of course you don't. But what I still don't understand is why you think any guy could possibly be interested in you."

"I don't. I don't think that at all." I get smaller and smaller with each word she utters, retreating into myself.

"Good. You shouldn't. And losing all that weight did nothing to make you more appealing. For the record, the all-black gothic shit you've got going on isn't helping either." She's looking down on me as she speaks, just like always—degrading and demeaning me in front of everyone.

"Just because he gives you a little attention doesn't mean he cares about you, anyway. Remember what happened the last time you thought someone wanted you?" she asks knowingly, reminding me of the past. "*Pathetic*. That's what you are, you know?" She finishes with a sinister smile, bumping into me as she walks away.

Groping blindly for the latch, I open my locker and bury my head inside, hoping to drown out the noise, taking the chance to gather myself. I may not be able to hold back the tears, but that doesn't mean I want everyone to see them.

Just a few more days. Just a few more weeks. You're almost done. You can do this, Dimah, I tell myself, repeating my mantra so I can make it through the next few days, the next few minutes. The laughter behind me is still going as the student body rejoices in the fact that I was put down. Again.

I take a deep breath. I feel like such an idiot for allowing myself to be belittled, for not standing up for myself.

Someone touches my shoulder, making me jump.

"Sorry, I didn't mean to scare you," Aron says, and I turn to face him slowly.

"It's fine."

"Your eyes are red. Are you okay?" He asks the question innocently, with a sweet and caring voice—but I can't help remembering Janice's words. This is no different than last year. Aron is *no different* than Jacob.

"Yep. I'm great," I tell him, closing my locker and walking away.

"Wait up!"

I walk to my motorcycle, hoping Aron stayed behind. I don't need him bringing more attention to me. Janice doesn't need any more ammunition to attack me.

"Stop," Aron says, grabbing my arm and turning me around to face him.

"Leave me alone," I respond, tears threatening to spill once again.

He scans my face. "What happened? What's going on?" I pull my arm away. "Nothing."

"It's clearly not nothing otherwise you wouldn't be crying right now!"

"I'm not crying." But as the words leave my mouth, a tear trails down my face, betraying me.

"Talk to me," he begs.

"I can't."

"You can if you want to. Please, talk to me," he presses again. I look behind him, seeing that once again we're drawing attention. Amid the crowd, I find Janice shooting daggers at me with her eyes. She looks at Aron, then back at me. Then she shakes her head and smiles deviously.

"No," I reply.

"Why not?"

"Because, you don't actually care. Nobody does."

"What did they do to you, Emerson?" he whispers. He looks back at the mass of students still watching us, wondering what the handsome quarterback could possibly want with the slutty, ugly girl.

"Like you don't already know," I whisper brokenly.

No Calm After the Storm

THE WEEKS FOLLOWING PROM WEREN'T PLEASANT. ACTUALLY, they were a living hell. Every time I walked by anyone, I'd get the dirty looks. The laughter. The fucking judgment.

I didn't expect my junior year to be this crappy. I didn't expect Jacob to be a horrible human being.

Speaking of Jacob, he hasn't said a thing to me since prom night. He took my virginity, made a joke of me in front of everyone, and let Janice make fun of me as much as she wanted.

Part of me hoped it was because he felt shitty about what he did, but I knew it was because I was the new pariah—the one no one wanted to be near. And to think I gave him a part of me I couldn't get back, a part I could never give to anyone else. Stupidly, I thought we were finally going to be happy together ...

"SWEETIE, ARE YOU OKAY?" MY MOM ASKS ME FROM ACROSS THE dinner table, shaking me from my thoughts.

"Fine," I say. But fine isn't really the truth. I am everything but fine. If I could walk around the school with earplugs to block out the noise without looking ridiculous, I would.

Headphones do most of the work for me, but since the school banned them from use indoors, there isn't much they can do to protect me from the sea of gossip I'm drowning in.

"Are you sure?" *she asks, waiting for confirmation.*

"Yep." *I lie to her face, ashamed. I wonder if she can tell.*

"Are you excited the year is coming to an end?" *She's desperately trying to make dinner time conversation—conversation I'm not inclined to have.*

"Yeah." *The truth this time—and that's the only response that has been genuine. School ending for the year means I won't see Jacob ever again, won't have to live with the constant reminder of how naïve I was. I won't have to look at the guy that took my entire reputation and flipped it on its ass.*

The source of my embarrassment. The reason I no longer participate in school activities.

The reason I wear big sweaters and sweatpants—because everyone wants to comment on my body.

The reason I don't speak with anyone, after realizing I had become a social outcast people wanted nothing to do with.

Yeah. I am fucking ecstatic that the year is about to end.

"Can I go to Grandma's for the summer?" *I ask, voicing the question that's been on my mind since I found out the truth.*

"The whole summer?" *she asks, looking a little conflicted.*

"Yes. I think it would do me good to get away." *To hide.*

"Get away from what?" *my mom questions.*

"Just this town." And the people in it, *I add in my mind.*

"I thought you loved this town."

"I do." *I did. But now, it's just too small. I don't think I can stand another summer of being around the same people—the same bullies. I don't think I'll survive it.*

"What's going on, Dimah?" my mother tries to coax me into telling her what's happening, but I refuse to answer.

"I just need a break, Mom. Especially before school starts again." I give her an easy tale, an answer she'll want to believe.

"I'll talk to your grandma," she promises—and for the first time in the last few weeks, I give her a semi-genuine smile. For the first time, I feel like the end of my suffering is in sight.

9

AND YOUR TONGUE COULD NOT GET ENOUGH.

Just before seventh period, I go over to the nurse's office and tell her I'm not feeling well. That just adds to my ever-growing list of lies, but I can't face Gym today—not after my last run-in with Janice, or the follow up with Aron.

"So, what's going on, Dimah?" Nurse Johnson asks.

"I'm not feeling too well."

"You said that when you walked into my office. What's the problem?"

I rack my brain for the next lie to tell. You'd think it would be easy to fabricate them by now, considering they've been my shield for the last few months—but every time I tell one, it chips away at what remains of who I am. Of who I was.

"Are you pregnant?" The nurse's words break through my internal thoughts.

"Am I what?" I ask, my voice rising.

"Are you pregnant?"

"Why would you say that?"

Not the End

"It's not like we don't know you're sexually active. The walls have ears." She looks at me like I should know. Like I should be aware of what a slut I am. As if I'm the only one who's missed the memo.

"Are you *serious?*" I ask, a laugh escaping my lips. It echoes around me—maniacal and wild—and it scares me.

She looks me up and down. "I know you slept with Jacob Hastings last year." I can see the disgust in her eyes, the way her nose wrinkles in disapproval. "I'm sure he isn't the only one," she adds.

My hands begin to shake; I start rocking back and forth on my heels, but she doesn't notice. She doesn't realize I'm a cup that's been filled to the brim and I'm about to overflow. She doesn't realize what her words are doing to me.

"You've gotta be fucking kidding me!" I shout, all restraint finally breaking.

She gives me a condescending smile. "Watch your language, sweetie. It'll be alright—some people just make poor choices," she says, trying to fucking *soothe* me.

I can't believe the nerve of this woman. Stupid high school students I could deal with. Teenagers with nothing better to do than make fun of me, I could get over. I could ignore it. I could live with it.

But not this.

Not an adult, without the slightest semblance of an idea of what actually happened, throwing it back in my face. This, for some reason, I cannot stand for.

A strength I haven't felt in years surges through my body; a sudden air of confidence comes over me, and a little piece of who I used to be before last year comes back to life. "You have no idea what you're talking about," I spit out.

"Honey, I think everyone knows what I'm talking about," she reasons. *The walls have ears* means she's listened to all the insults thrown my way on the daily. She's heard all the things I've been called, all the things that have been said. And she's done nothing. As a nurse, she has a duty to care for her students; I'm both shocked and disgusted by the realization that she's chosen to ignore that responsibility. Clearly, like everyone else, she prefers to pass judgment on me for choices I *didn't* have.

"You should be wary of taking the words of high school students as gospel."

"What do you mean?"

"It means that not everything you hear is true."

"Some of it is," she says.

"Some of it isn't."

"So, you're saying you didn't sleep with Jacob and all the other guys I keep hearing about?"

I pause for a second. "All the other guys?" I ask. "Yeah, the other football players from last year. Some people in band. You've been getting around, apparently."

My hands flex into fists. "Do they teach staff to blame the victim too?" I ask in a low voice.

"Victim? You?" she says in surprise, like me being a victim is so far-fetched she can't believe it.

"You should've asked, like you're supposed to do. But I guess the rumor mill's too entertaining."

The nurse sniffs. "It happens. People sleep with other people. Sometimes they regret it later. I just wanted to make sure you weren't coming in here because you're pregnant. You should know how to be safe by now."

"Why don't you just shut up?"

She frowns. "Excuse me?"

"You insist on speaking about something you know nothing about."

"I know enough." She crosses her arms, looking down on me.

"Bullshit. You know nothing. You know only what you've been spoon fed."

"Most rumors are at least a little bit true, Dimah."

"You're really bad at your job."

"I'm doing my job. Checking on whether students are having unprotected sex is a part of it."

"I guess you can only manage one thing at a time then, and poorly at that."

Prom Night

HE UNZIPS MY DRESS, PULLING MY HAIR, KISSING ME ROUGHLY. I imagine what it would be like if it were happening slowly, if it were sweet instead of rushed. But regardless of how much I close my eyes and try to envision it all happening differently, the taste of alcohol on his lips is a reminder—this is my reality.

"Stop," I tell him, pulling away as he tightens his grip on me.

He doesn't listen. He continues to kiss me, pulling my hair painfully as his hands travel over my body. He moves towards the bed, pulling me along with him. Suddenly, he rips my dress open.

I watch it fall slowly to the floor. "Jacob," *I whisper, a tear gliding down my face.*

"Isn't this what you've wanted for a long time?" *he asks me.*

I finally notice the slurring of his words, the redness in his eyes. He's looking at me like a predator looks at its prey. "Not like this," *I tell him.*

It doesn't derail his focus. He pushes me down on the bed, rips off my underwear.

"Stop." *I hear myself shouting in my head—but there aren't any words coming out of my mouth.* Stop! Stop! Stop! *I keep shouting but...he doesn't stop.*

He doesn't ask me if I'm enjoying this. He doesn't check to see if I'm okay. He never even looks at me—not even as he takes the part of me that no one else has had.

It ends in a matter of seconds, but to me it feels like hours.

Maybe he just got too lost in the moment. Maybe it was the alcohol that caused him to be so aggressive.

Maybe he really likes me and this was his way of showing it.

Maybe next time he'll be sweet.

Maybe next time he'll listen.

Maybe next time... he'll ask.

10

YET, LOSING ME, FOR YOU AND ME WAS NOT THE SAME.

I rush out of the room like there's fire under my feet. I don't give the nurse a second glance. No more words. Nothing. She isn't the problem anyway—not the main problem, that is. She just did what everyone else does. She bought into the gossip, believed the lies. She's nothing more than the tail of the snake, and cutting off the tail will do nothing to stop the poison.

I walk around the school, waiting for my anger to subside.

Just breathe in. Breathe out. Repeat.

I continue to guide myself through that simple motion, hoping it'll loosen the building tension in my chest...but I still feel it. I'm still suffocating under the weight, and it's only increasing with each inhalation.

I walk over to my locker to get the books I need to take home with me. Above my head, the bell rings, followed closely by doors opening, pounding footsteps, increasing noise. I block out all the chatter, trying the combination to my locker again since my first attempt failed. I do it slowly this time, carefully, because the shaking in my hand isn't helping.

Calm down. Not this. Not right now, Dimah, I tell myself as I finish the combination and pull the lock down. Just as I'm about to open the door, a hand comes from behind me and slams it shut again.

"I'm glad you followed my advice and backed off." Janice's voice echoes in my ears.

"Leave me alone," I tell her, my tone eerily calm.

"What did you just say?" she says, spinning me around and pressing me against the locker.

"I said, you should leave me alone," I repeat. My voice shakes, revealing the strength of my emotions.

Janice smirks. "Did you guys hear that?" she asks the crowd loudly. "The school slut is telling me to back off!" Pinning me with her sharp gaze, she drawls, "Or what? What are you going to do if I don't?" A small, inarticulate sound comes out of my mouth. She laughs—*everyone* laughs. She digs her fingers into my shoulder, pressing me against the wall of lockers.

I look down at her hand, feeling my own twitch in response. "I'm not going to say it again," I warn her, my voice low enough for only her to hear.

Her top lip curls slightly before she announces to the crowd, "Did you guys hear that? Easy Girl isn't going to say it again."

Deep breath, Dimah, I tell myself. I inhale deeply, then release the breath. "I'm done taking your shit," I tell her, bringing both hands to Janice's shoulders and shoving her as hard as I can to the other side of the hall.

"Oooh, the slut has a temper!" someone yells in the crowd.

"Did you see that?" someone else adds.

"What the fuck do you think you're doing?" Janice says, climbing to her feet.

"I told you to back off."

"You think you're tough now?" she asks, charging at me. I brace myself for the punching that will follow, the pulling of hair, the inevitable fight—but it doesn't come.

"Let me go!" Janice shouts.

I look up to see Aron with his arms around her waist, stopping her from getting closer to me. Janice looks behind her and smiles, no longer fighting, seemingly content that he's gotten close to her.

"What's going on here?" Aron's voice booms in the hallway; everyone falls silent.

"Dimah is off her meds, apparently," Janice whines. "Picking fights with me just because I'm telling her the truth."

"Shut the fuck up," I demand. I swear I hear everyone gasp.

Aron's eyes find mine and he asks, "Dimah, are you okay?" I look at him and don't know what to think. Is he holding her because he wants to protect her, or is he holding her because he wants to protect me?

"Okay? You're asking if *she's* okay?" Janice shrieks. "That bitch pushed me! You should be asking if *I'm* okay."

"I told you to leave me alone."

"Like you left Jacob alone? Despite knowing he didn't like you, you followed him around like a lost puppy. And when you got the opportunity, you screwed him, slut."

"You know, for someone who claims to know so much, you don't know shit." I take a step closer to her.

"Excuse me, whore?" Janice sneers.

"You've been so intent on calling me names, so intent on making me look bad for sleeping with your boyfriend, but you're the one I feel bad for."

"Oh, please. You feel bad for me?" she scoffs.

"Yes, *you*. Because you allowed your boyfriend to rape someone for the sake of a dumb fucking high school game. And then you took him back. *That's* pathetic." Silence. My declaration is met with shocked faces and deafening silence. "You focused so much on how easy I was...I guess it didn't matter that I never agreed to it."

"You're lying," Janice spits.

Now it's my turn to scoff—at *her* ignorance, at *her* naiveté. "I said yes to going to prom. I was foolish to think he liked me, but that was all. I never wanted to sleep with him. And I told him that much—as he forced himself on me and made prom the worst day of my life."

"Stop lying," Janice shouts. Aron's still holding her back, but his eyes are focused on mine. I see a storm of anger brewing in his gaze as he stands there, frozen.

"I'm not lying. Whether you believe me or not is up to you, but I'm sick and tired of you..." I pause and look around the hall full of students before adding, "and your sick, mindless followers, calling me names behind my back, making my life impossible—speaking without knowing."

I walk toward her slowly, sizing her up. I know that to her, and likely everyone else in the room, it appears that I've transformed before their eyes. Some may even think

I've lost my mind for standing up to someone like Janice. But I haven't lost my mind at all—in fact, I think I've gained a piece of it back.

It's the part of me that wants me to fight for myself, the part that will no longer allow me to be a doormat.

I close the distance, so close now that we're face-to-face. "If you so much as whisper my name again, I swear I will drag your pathetic, self-centered ass through these halls."

"You wouldn't dare," Janice challenges.

"You have no idea what I'd do. You don't *know me*. You only know the person you created through the venom you spewed—but I promise you I can be much worse." I look to Aron. "Let her go."

Hesitantly, he releases her.

"You're crazy. He didn't rape you," she says, shaking her head and looking around at the students surrounding us. They look back, their eyes full of questions.

I shrug. "Tell yourself that if it's what you need to hear. But I was there, and you weren't. Now, are you going to back off, or do I have to make you?" I ask, staring down at her, stepping closer. As close as we are now, I realize I'm taller than she is; another piece of who I used to be clicks back into place—stronger this time.

Janice looks around the room again, and then at Aron, still standing at her side. She knows she's lost this battle; she never expected me to fight back. I needed to cut the head off the snake though, and she's the head.

I hear the shuffling of feet, and cautiously tear my gaze away from Janice to survey the room. Everyone has shifted positions; they're all standing behind me now.

The only people on the other side of the room are Janice and Aron.

I let out a short, triumphant laugh. Lines have been drawn and now that the truth is out, most people are with me; it's funny how the tide has turned, how things have changed. Most of these people have talked about me behind my back for so long I almost can't remember a better time—but now, their eyes show empathy. Guilt. Sorrow. Embarrassment.

I turn to Janice again, tapping my foot. "I'm waiting."

"If you knew she'd been attacked and didn't say anything, I'll make sure you regret it for the rest of your life." Aron's voice echoes off the walls as he walks away from her, making his way towards me. Standing at my side, he rests his hand gently on the small of my back.

"I didn't know," she whispers.

"Dimah won't be the only one making your life hell if you mess with her again. I will come after you too. And you wouldn't want that." By the time he finishes speaking, Aron's voice is hardly more than a growl. Janice flinches visibly.

She looks at me, then at Aron, her eyes scanning over everyone else behind us. A lone tear slides down her cheek; she seems to become smaller right in front of my eyes, and I can sense her powerlessness.

The same powerlessness I've been living in ever since prom night.

Then, she does exactly what the old me would have done—she turns toward the exit and runs. As she disappears, another piece of my puzzle slips back into place.

11

LOSING ME, FOR YOU WAS THE BEGINNING.

All I needed was the courage to take ownership of my life. Telling everyone in the room what happened wasn't ideal, but I wasn't thinking about that in the moment. All I knew was that the weight wasn't going to go away until I did something about it.

The words of my peers weren't going to stop hurting me until I said a few of my own.

I don't know what's going to happen to Jacob now—but honestly, I don't intend to waste another thought on it. Maybe there'll be a trial in the future. Maybe not. All I know is that people who do bad things eventually pay for what they've done.

"Hey Emerson, wait up!" I hear Aron say as I make my way to my bike.

"What's up?" I ask. It's great to be feeling so much more relaxed than I was at the beginning of the week; it's great not to suffocate under the need to hide anymore. I walk with my head up and my chin high. In the days after my confrontation with Janice, I've gone to class, my locker, the cafeteria—and I haven't heard anything negative being said. I haven't heard anything being said at all.

"Could we..." he stops and runs his fingers through his hair. "Want to give me that motorcycle ride now?"

"Right now?" I ask him. I haven't seen him since Friday when I finally stood up to Janice—he tried to talk to me after I was done, but I asked him for some space. I can only slay one dragon at a time.

"No time like the present," he says with a smile.

"Okay," I respond. I might as well face this now rather than later.

He looks shocked. "Really?"

"I'm feeling particularly courageous today, so why not?" Actually, I can think of a few reasons, but I'm not sure if they're real or not so for now, I'll ignore them.

"Cool. Um...there's a really cool place I want to take you to," he says, frowning slightly.

I fold my arms across my chest. "I said courageous, but I'm not sure it extends quite *that* far."

"You'll love it," he says nervously.

The badgered me cowers away because I've heard similar promises before—but the stronger, bolder, *former* me steps up to the plate. "Okay."

"I'll give you directions as you drive."

I hop on my bike; Aron climbs on behind me. He slides his hands around my waist to hold onto me, and the butterflies in my stomach launch into somersault mode. I knew this guy would be trouble.

Then again, he's been nothing but nice to me, even helping me out when I confronted Janice. He didn't have to say what he did to her, didn't have to have my back.

But he did.

Maybe I can be friends with him.

Maybe he deserves a chance.

"Pull over here," Aron shouts, leaning closer to be heard over the wind.

"Right here?" I yell back.

"Yes!"

I pull over next to a field full of flowers in the middle of nowhere. "What is this place?" I ask, taking off my helmet.

"It's one of my favorite spots." "Really?"

"Yeah. I spent a lot of time here last year."

I can tell there's more to that statement—a story he's maybe not willing to share right now.

"Follow me," he says, moving into the field. He walks through the flowers until he reaches the middle, then shrugs off his bag and drops it on the ground. Unzipping it, he retrieves a blanket.

Stepping back warily, I cross my arms over my chest. "You had a blanket in there this whole time?"

He peers up at me, smiling. "I've had it for a few days now."

"I guess you really do like coming here."

"I haven't been in a while," he answers, shrugging.

"So, you carry the blanket just in case you need it?"

"I carried it because I was hoping you'd say yes to coming here with me."

"That's a little presumptuous," I joke.

"More like hopeful."

"Why did you want to bring me here?" I ask, watching him as he opens the blanket and spreads it carefully. He motions for me to take a seat; cautiously, I do.

He sits down with me, his eyes searching mine before he speaks. "Before last week, you kept asking me why I was interested in talking to you," he says carefully.

"I'm actually still wondering."

"I understand why you kept questioning my intentions now. I had heard a little about last year."

The little bit of peace I found on the ride here is instantly gone. He heard the whispers. This is why he's interested in me. He thinks I'm easy. "Of course you did."

"I didn't know it was you."

"You must have. Unless you live under a rock, you couldn't have missed the rumors."

"I wasn't really in school most of last year—when I finally started coming, I was too angry to focus on anyone or anything."

"But this year? You've heard the rumors. How could you not know they were about me?"

"I've heard chatter here and there. I didn't know it was about you when I first talked to you outside the dance."

"So, why did you talk to me?"

"Because you reminded me of what I turned into last year," he answers. He looks away, taking in the beauty of the field. Clearly, last year isn't something he likes to talk about. Which is fine—it's not something I like to talk about either.

"When did you start hearing them?" I ask.

"I was in the locker room getting ready for a game. I

Not the End

heard one of the players talk about the rites of passage—and last year's tasks." I can hear the disappointment in his voice. "I couldn't believe some of the shit they did. They were looking forward to it this year, too. I was sick to my stomach when they talked about you hooking up with Jacob."

When he says 'hooking up,' I flinch. I can't help it.

"I'm sorry. I know that's not what happened. I just wish I knew sooner. I would've made him pay for what he did, Dimah. I *wanted* to make him pay anyway for using you to fulfill a fucking task. I couldn't understand why someone like you would want to be with him in the first place, and then to hear what he did to you?" He spits out each word, pain and anger lacing the tone of his voice.

"It's over now," I tell him.

"It shouldn't have happened—and it *won't* happen again. I told the coaches about the stupid tasks on that list a while ago, and now it's been banned. Any student suspected of doing that shit will be expelled immediately."

"That's a relief," I say, a little flabbergasted by his declaration.

"I wish I could have done more," he says. He reaches for my hand, but pulls away at the last minute. My disappointment at his retreat surprises me.

"You didn't know me."

"I didn't, but I wanted to. Even last year. I'd see you walking around school with a cardigan, jeans and a T-shirt, and your nose always buried in a book. I always wondered what you were really like."

"So how come you never said anything?" Why had he never approached me before?

"Because I was in a bad place last year. But then—at the dance—I decided to stop being a coward and come talk to you." He takes a deep breath and adds, "I don't blame you for thinking I was another asshole trying to take advantage of you. I'm a football player too, so I see why you'd think that I had a task to fulfill. But I want you to understand that's not the case. I've actually liked you for a long time now."

"Liked me?" I ask, waiting for him to correct himself.

"Yes," he says with a smile. "I know you don't know me very well, but I'd like you to. I'd like to get to know you, too. Actually, I'd like to date you."

"Why?" My tone drips with surprise.

He chuckles, shaking his head. "Because you're strong. You're beautiful and smart and funny. You're the only girl in that school I've ever imagined myself with, and when I saw you wear my jersey, despite how angry I was that those girls treated you like that, I couldn't help but wonder what it would be like to be with you. To share more than my jersey with you."

I blush. "Now you're just saying random things."

"They aren't random. They're true."

"So, you want to date me?"

"I'd like to—but only if you like the idea as much as I do."

I point back and forth between us, saying, "Me, date you?"

"Jeez, Emerson. Yes! Maybe today wasn't the right day

to ask you, but I got sick of waiting for the right day," he says.

I can't help it; I smile because I can't hold it back. "I feel a little more like my old self today," I tell him. I've been feeling like my old self more and more with each passing day—but my old self has definitely been mixed with some new parts.

New confidence. New strength.

"I can see that." He takes hold of my hand and a sense of comfort overtakes me. "I'm so proud of you for standing up for yourself."

Goosebumps spread up my arm. "Thank you for pushing me to do it," I answer. "You were right about what would happen if I just stood up for myself."

"I wanted to fight your battle for you, but I know from experience that the only way you'd find yourself again—find that girl I used to watch walking the halls—was if you fought for yourself."

"You were right. It was my fight to win."

"And that you did." I can see the pride in his eyes as the words leave his mouth. He takes a deep breath and adds, "So, about that date?" He runs his fingers through his hair once again, and I realize he's nervous.

"It sort of feels like we're on a date right now," I respond, feeling my cheeks redden.

"In that case, I've brought some food too," Aron says, grabbing his bag and opening it up once again.

I laugh as he pulls out some containers. "You really came prepared!"

"What can I say? I'm an optimistic man."

I smile. "A little bit of optimism never hurt anyone."

. . .

WE SPEND A FEW MORE HOURS OUT IN THE FIELD, EATING the food he made, telling each other stories. I get to know him a little more, and he gets to know me too—the real me. We take our time. Nothing is rushed and everything is perfect, just as I imagined it would be. He treats me the way I thought no one else would. Afterwards, I drive him back to school to pick up his car, then he tails me home to be sure I make it there safely. We sit on the steps of my house and talk a little longer, laugh a little louder.

At the end of the night, when the street lights come on, we linger at my front door. My eyes flutter closed as his lips find my forehead and he places the sweetest of kisses there. He embraces me briefly, then watches as I open the door to head inside.

Perfect.

Aron Lincoln might just be the man I deserve.

And this right here? This is just the beginning of our story. It's not the end.

EPILOGUE

BUT LOSING ME, FOR ME WAS THE END.

Six Months Later...

I told Mom everything. I started at the beginning, from the moment Jacob asked me to prom, to everything that happened at school in the time since.

She cried, apologizing profusely.

I'll never forget the look on her face the moment I let go and cried on her lap, the moment I finally shared everything I'd been holding onto. She looked distraught.

But I was finally okay.

Our tears kept coming while we held onto each other. I told her it wasn't her fault; she said she should have pressed me more. I told her it would have been pointless because I wasn't ready to do anything about it.

Not until the day the school nurse judged me, too.

JANICE STILL GRADUATED. SHE'S SOMEWHERE, FURTHERING

her education, but she'll likely always play the role of the mean girl. The last I heard, Jacob got kicked out of the football program he'd been accepted into for questionable behavior. There's chatter about legal action being brought against him.

I know everyone will get what they deserve.

I definitely got what I deserved...

"Where did you go?" Aron's question brings my attention back to the present. I watch the sun begin to set as we drive along a quiet stretch of road.

"Just thinking about this past year," I tell him.

"Are you okay?" I can see his concern for me before he returns his eyes to the road ahead.

"I am." And while I'm not one hundred percent yet, I'm well on my way. The pieces of who I used to be are finally coming together. I'm not a finished puzzle, but I'm better than I used to be.

"Good," he says, and I can sense his relief.

"Thank you. For everything," I tell him, squeezing his hand.

"You don't need to thank me. I didn't do anything, honestly; I'll always be sorry for that."

"You didn't know." I know if he did, he'd have done something—that's just the kind of person he is.

"I would've known if I hadn't had my head up my ass." He shakes his head, disgusted.

"You were battling your own demons," I assure him.

"That doesn't mean I shouldn't have noticed yours."

Not the End

I frown, watching his profile as he drives. "I fight my own battles."

"That you do. You're strong, Em," he says tightening his grip on my hand.

"You're not so bad yourself, Lincoln," I tell him jokingly.

"Ready for this?" he asks, as we head down I-95 toward the future—our future.

I'm definitely nervous—but I pull myself together enough to say, "I'm sort of ready. Are you?"

"Bragan University won't even know what hit them," he says with a chuckle.

We're silent for a moment, just riding together. "Did you think—after that day you talked to me outside the dance—that we'd be heading to college together right now?" I ask, curious to hear his answer. I didn't expect to be here, didn't expect to move forward, to move on.

"I didn't think we'd be here, no, but I'm so glad we are."

"You and me both," I tell him with a smile.

"If I had a drink, I'd toast to a new beginning."

"To a new beginning, indeed."

I got myself back.

And I got Aron Lincoln. Everything else will fall in line.

Make sure you grab Not the Same and dive into Aron Lincoln's Story!

LOSING ME
ROSA ANGELA RAMOS

I know this emotion too well.

I, too, have lost me many times before.

But unlike you, I needed to find me to survive.

Unlike you, losing the palm of my hands to the brightness of the sun meant the earth stopped rotating around my
thighs.

Losing me, for me meant the stars stopped shining life into the darkness of my skin.

Losing the goodness my mama poured into my heart as she gave life to me.

But for you, losing me was like drinking tea without honey.

Losing Me

Easy to replace with sugar.

Though, we both know I taste purely sweet like sugarcane.

And your tongue could not get enough.

Yet, losing me, for you and me was not the same.

Losing me, for you was the beginning. But losing me, for me was the end.

AUTHOR'S NOTE

I have a friend who has a tattoo of a semicolon. I asked her, "why?". She responded by reminding me that a semicolon is used to separate major sentence elements. She says it indicated to her the start of something new after the end of a previous event.

She said it reminded her that her story was not over; rather, it was just taking a different direction.

Dimah Emerson took over my thoughts. I wasn't even done writing the next book in my series when she swept through and demanded to be written. I wrote more in a day than I have ever written before.

She was a slow brewing storm. And then she finally blew up.

Dimah Emerson represents—at least to me—every young girl who has been bullied, misunderstood, made fun of, assaulted, and put down. Dimah Emerson represents so many of us. I didn't expect this story to go where it went; initially, it was supposed to be just bullying, but she took it in a different direction and I couldn't ignore it.

Author's Note

This story is about her. This story is about all of us.

Dimah lived with her head down for a little while. She changed who she was in response to what was going on around her and what happened to her. She became a shell of the person she used to be. She lost herself.

I hope this story motivates you to find yourself.

Dimah needed to find herself, to take ownership of her life in order to move forward. She couldn't just sit there and let the things that happened to her keep her down.

I hope to one day have some of the courage she has. I hope one day you share her courage too.

NOT THE SAME

NOT ALONE NOVELLAS, BOOK 2

Not the Same

He was left with no choice.

NOT ALONE NOVELLAS
GIANNA GABRIELA

Not the Same

GIANNA GABRIELA

COPYRIGHT

Not the Same

Not Alone Novellas (Book Two) Copyright © 2018 Gianna Gabriela

ISBN Ebook: 978-1951325008

ISBN Print: 978-1792143892

All rights reserved. No part of this book may be reproduced or transmitted in any form, including electronic or mechanical, or by any other means, without written permission from the author. The only time passages may be used is for teasers, blog posts, articles, or reviews, so long as the work isn't being wrongfully used.

This book is a work of fiction. Characters, names, places, events, and incidents portrayed are solely from the author's imagination. Any resemblance to actual places, people, events, or other incidents is coincidental or are used fictitiously.

Editor: Lauren Dawes

Cover design & formatting by Sly Fox Cover Designs

DEDICATION

To those of you struggling with responsibilities you shouldn't be shouldering. Know that you are strong. You are capable. You are seen. You are enough.

Yours,
Gianna

PROLOGUE

I WISH DAD WAS HERE.

"Hey, Mom, what's this?" I ask, holding up a small plastic bag. I found it inside one of her shoes in the closet when I was playing hide and seek with Ethan. "Is it sugar?" Maybe she forgot it was there. I know she's planning on making lemonade today.

"Where did you find that, Aron?" she asks. She sounds like she's mad, but I don't understand why; she's usually happy when I find things.

"It was—"

She runs to me, prying the bag from my hand. "Where did you find it?" she yells and my bottom lip begins to tremble. I look down to see there's a little bit of blood on my hand. I think she scratched me when she snatched the bag away.

Tears begin to stream down my face. "It was in your..." I mumble, not understanding what I did to make Mom so mad.

"Where?" she shouts and I flinch.

"Closet," I reply. Ethan stayed in the room. He's hiding until I go and find him. I'm glad he's not here to see me cry.

"Don't go in there again!"

"We were just playing hide and seek," I say.

She gives me a look that tells me I'm in trouble. "Don't *ever* go in my closet again." She says each word slowly and I nod, lips still trembling, tears still falling.

I don't know what I did to make her mad.

She's not usually mad at me.

I wish Dad was here.

She was never angry when he was here.

1

I SHOULDN'T BE THE ONE PARENTING THE PARENT.

Five years later...

I walk into my house, angry and ready to confront my mother for leaving Ethan at school for two extra hours. She's supposed to pick him up when I have football practice. That's her *one* job—the one thing I let her do, but she even fails at that. When I showed up, the principal gave me a look of pity and my little brother gave me a hug. Ethan was scared. He'd been crying and I could only imagine how many scenarios ran through his little head—none of them close to the reality I walk in to.

Just as I suspected, and the reason I told Ethan to wait for me in his room, my mother is sitting at the kitchen table with white powder spread out on the surface in front of her.

"What are you doing?" I ask in disgust. I've caught her doing this enough times to know exactly what it is, but I ask anyway, hoping the answer will be different this time.

"What are *you* doing here? I thought you had practice?" she asks, changing the subject. I drop my gym bag onto the floor. The disappointment I feel should be obvious to her, but I think she's oblivious—or perhaps used to it—by now.

I watch her try to put the rest of the white powder—the evidence of her wrongdoing— back into the bag. "I did have practice."

"So why aren't you there now?" Her tone is accusatory. Only my mother would dare question my actions when hers are less than legal. She puts the small bag inside her jeans pocket.

"The school called," I say, counting the seconds until she realizes what she did this time.

Ten seconds.

Ten whole seconds.

"Shit, Ethan!" she says, finally remembering.

Anger is coursing through my blood. "You were supposed to pick him up *two hours* ago."

She looks over my shoulder. "Where is he now?"

"Upstairs doing homework, not that you actually care."

"I do care!" she snarls in reply.

I look at her intently. "Really? *You* care? Since when?" I spit out. I shouldn't be the one parenting the parent. This wasn't supposed to be my job.

"I'm your mother," she argues weakly.

I scoff. She hasn't been a mother to us in years. I had to raise myself—and Ethan too. "Is that what you want to call yourself now? Because you seem to be forgetting what your role is."

Suddenly contrite, she approaches me, framing my

Not the Same

face with her palms. "I forgot, okay?" she says softly. I place my hands on top of hers, prying them from my face. I won't give her the absolution she seeks.

"Yes, you did." *You forgot you're a parent, that you have children, that you shouldn't be doing drugs. You can't forget your kid at school for two hours because you're too busy getting high.*

These are all the things I want to tell her, but I don't.

Because I've said it all before to no avail.

I guess she also forgot how to listen.

"Dude, you can't quit!" George says as I pack my things from the men's locker room.

I sigh. Mom has forgotten to pick Ethan up not once —but every day this week. I can't keep leaving practice early to go and get him. "I have no choice."

I know Coach understands, since he's the only one who has even a vague idea of what my home life is like, but I can't keep doing this to the team. A quarterback is one of the really important pieces on the board—a piece that needs to remain constant.

"You're the quarterback," Tyler says. He doesn't understand my situation—probably because I haven't said anything. To anyone. I'm too ashamed.

I shake my head. "Not anymore."

"What about the college scholarship?" George asks.

"I'll have to aim for a merit one instead," I reason. The truth is, a college scholarship won't matter because there's no way I'll be allowed to bring Ethan to the dorms with me. And I can't afford to live off campus with him while going to school.

The best I can do is graduate high school and get a job so I can get a small place for us.

Maybe when Ethan finishes high school and goes to college, I can think about college for myself.

"Really? A merit scholarship?" Tyler says, laughing.

I punch him in the shoulder. "I have straight As!"

"Dude, watch the arm. *You* may be done with football, but *I* can't get injured if we're going to try and not get killed this season because of the second-string quarterback you're leaving us with."

"He's not so bad," I tell them.

Tyler and George open their lockers in unison, staring at me in disbelief.

"Not that bad?" George says. "The guy can't complete a pass!"

"The dude freaks out when he sees players running his way," Tyler adds.

"No quarterback wants to get sacked," I say. It's true. Not everyone can take a hit either.

I look at my uniform, my number and name on the back. I'm going to miss doing this. Playing football was my shelter from the chaos that is my life, but it's time to grow up. I've got someone else I have to protect. Although I love football, I love my brother a lot more.

"I'm just saying, we're about to hit a dry spell," George says and we all laugh. It's not like we've been winning every game; we're a worthy opponent, but far from having a perfect season.

"Let's just hope it's a short one," Tyler says, picking up his bag from the bench and tossing it in his locker.

"So, no practice for you today?" George asks.

I shut my locker. "Dude, I'm not playing football anymore. Why would I go to practice?" I look down at my watch—I've got to be at Ethan's school in a few minutes for pick up.

Tyler shoves George and gives him an *are you serious?* look.

"I gotta go," I tell them.

"We'll miss playing with you," Tyler says, never afraid to voice his thoughts.

"We're still friends," I assure them.

"Since we *are* friends, I'm throwing a party next weekend. My parents will be away. We can celebrate, or commiserate over, your departure from the team. You better be there!" George says.

"I'll try and show for a couple of hours," I tell him, knowing it won't happen. There's no way I'm going to leave Ethan alone with Mom so I can go off and party.

2

SHE DOESN'T ASK HOW I'M DOING

It's been a week since I quit football and I miss it so much. It was my one outlet and now it's gone. Instead, I'm stuck having to mitigate the impact my mom's drug habit has on my little brother's life. When I arrive home, I can hear the sound of furniture being moved or dumped onto the floor.

"What did you do?" Richard barks at me as I walk in.

I look at him with disdain. "What are you talking about?" I ask, pretending not to have a clue.

He closes the distance between us one step at a time. "You *know* what I'm talking about."

I defy him because if it weren't for him, we probably wouldn't be in this place right now—my mom wouldn't be in this place.

I shrug casually. "Nope, no clue." Turning around, I head to my room but I don't make it two steps before I'm slammed against the wall.

Richard leans in close to my ear, his forearm on the back of my neck pinning me in place. "Where did you put it?" he demands in a slow drawl. When I remain silent, he grabs my shoulder and spins me around. Trapped between him and the wall, I feel the rage pounding through my blood. I want to hit him so badly.

But I hold back.

"Where?" he shouts. Richard glares at me with red-rimmed eyes. Still, I say nothing. With a frustrated growl, he brings both of his hands to my throat, wrapping his fingers around tightly until he cuts off my air.

I gasp loudly, my breath barely a whisper when I say, "Trash."

"You threw it in the *fucking* trash?"

He lets me go, walking to the kitchen. I hear him upending the trash bag, looking for the drugs responsible for destroying my family.

Tough shit.

I walk over to where he is, watching as he searches for something he won't find. "Where are they?" he shouts, briefly turning to me before returning to his search. I look towards the yard through the kitchen window.

Richard follows my gaze. "God dammit," he breathes. I don't know why I'm still standing here, watching him look for it. This might not end well for me, but I don't care.

Not today.

Richard throws open the door to the backyard, yanking it so hard it comes off its hinges. Mentally, I count down how long it'll take for him to return empty-handed. A devious grin appears on my face as I picture him going through the trash with his bare hands, searching for his precious drugs.

It's too bad I flushed them all down the toilet.

"What the fuck did you do with them?" he shouts, stepping back into the kitchen.

"Oh, wait, you mean your *drugs?*" I ask.

"Yes," he says through gritted teeth.

"I thought you were asking about something else."

"What *else* would I be asking about? Where are they?"

"I flushed those down the toilet," I answer and pain radiates from my mouth. Richard hits me a second time, blood pouring from my split lip. Fisting my shirt with both hands, he throws me down onto the floor and kicks me in the ribs.

"You bastard! Do you know how much that was worth?" he asks, kicking me again.

One kick.

Two.

Three.

With an inarticulate scream, he turns around, grabbing his hair desperately. As quietly as I can, I get up from the floor and sneak up behind him. With lightning speed, I wrap my arm around his throat, tightening my grip as he begins to struggle. Richard tries to pry me off, but I'm stronger than he is—I have been for a while.

I let him get some hits in today, but he had to know it was my choice. For some reason, I wanted to hurt—to feel that pain, but now I'm going to hurt him.

"What the...? Aron stop right now!" my mother screams, rushing to help Richard.

"What's going on?" I hear someone say.

Ethan.

What's he doing here? It's the middle of the day?

Not the Same

I know he sees the blood running down my face.

I know he sees the way I'm holding Richard.

The way Richard is struggling.

I look at him and feel his fear.

I can see every question running through his mind and I'm angry at myself for putting them there in the first place.

I almost don't feel my mother pulling at me, hitting me, begging me to let go of Richard. I'm numb to it all.

"You're bleeding, Aron."

Those are the words that break me, tearing me from my frozen state. My little brother's words laced with concern and confusion are what cause me to let go of Richard altogether.

Richard drops to the floor, holding his neck and gasping for air. My mother falls down beside him, asking him how he's doing, if he's okay.

She ignores me, though.

She ignores the fact that I'm bleeding.

Richard has all of her attention.

"I'm okay, buddy." I try to assure Ethan but I feel like I've somehow torn up his image of me. I've disappointed him and that hurts me more than the punches and kicks Richard had rained on me earlier.

I'm an idiot.

I got carried away trying to piss off Richard.

"What are you doing out of school so soon?" I ask, wiping the blood from my face.

He ignores my question. "Why are you fighting?"

"I was just showing Richard something I learned—we're not really fighting."

He reaches up to touch my mouth, but I pull away. "You're bleeding," he says.

"Oh... I fell earlier and didn't wipe it off." I hate that I'm lying to him but I don't want him to think the worst of me.

"I don't want you to fight, even if it's make believe," he says innocently.

"Okay, I promise I won't," I assure him, guiding him up the stairs to his room and away from Mom and Richard. "So why are you home so early?"

"Water was falling all over the classroom."

"A pipe broke?" I ask.

"Yeah, they called Mom."

"Did she pick you up?"

He shakes his head. "No, Lance's mom brought me," he responds and that makes more sense to me.

"I'm gonna go get cleaned up and when I get back, we can go somewhere special," I tell him, praying I can erase what he's just witnessed.

"Are we going for ice cream?" he asks, hopeful.

"Ice cream and somewhere else too!"

He nods eagerly, and I take that as my chance to walk out of his room and compose myself. I don't want to be the reason for his nightmares.

3

I SCREAM AT THE TOP OF MY LUNGS, LETTING OUT ALL THE
FRUSTRATION, THE ANGER, THE PAIN

"Are you going to try it or not?" George asks me from his seat on the couch. I decided to come to his party after all, especially since Ethan is sleeping over at his friend Lance's house.

George's parents are out of town for the weekend, and they trusted their seventeen-year-old to stay at home and not throw a party. Big mistake.

The house has so many people in it that his parents wouldn't know what hit them if they dared come home early. I take another gulp of my beer and set it down on the table.

I shake my head. "Nah, I'm good."

"You gotta try it at least once," Tyler shouts over the music, taking a hit of the joint in question.

"Seriously, dude. Try it and then you can check it off your list," George says, trying to persuade me. Drugs aren't on my list, but I've always wondered what makes them so attractive.

What makes them so good that my mother gives in to them every other day?

"Screw it," I mutter under my breath. "Pass it over."

Some would call it peer pressure; I'd call it research.

"Just remember: inhale, hold, and then release," Tyler says, coaching me through it.

"Whatever." I take a hit, holding it for as long as I can. When I release it though, I start coughing like crazy.

"Dude, breathe," George says, laughing.

"Shut up," I respond, still unable to stop myself from coughing. I grab my beer from the table and down it.

"The first time always sucks. Want to try it again?" George asks, looking down at the joint I'm trying to give back to him. I stare at it intently, basking in the sensation of floating that washes over me. I know my mom's drug of choice is cocaine and sometimes heroin—whatever's available, but that's not what she started with. This was. The thought hits me out of nowhere, regret consuming me just as quickly.

"I'm good," I say, coming to my senses. I told myself I'd never smoke. I'd never give in to the master that controls my mother. Feeling like I betrayed not only myself but Ethan as well, I get up and go to the kitchen. I need to breathe for a minute. I grab another beer from the cooler, pop it open, and down it in one go.

I know it's probably a little hypocritical to say no to drugs, and then drink alcohol but I need something to take the edge off. I need to forget what it's like to walk in on my mother with a needle in her arm or with her nose to the table.

I take a second beer out of the cooler—feeling myself calming down—and join the guys back on the couch.

I swallow the rest of my drink, feeling the buzz trickle through my body, numbing me. I try to focus on the room, on the way people are dancing together, making out with each other. I don't know how much time passes before I feel someone walk their fingers up my chest. I turn, finding a girl seated in my lap.

When the hell did that happen?

I don't entirely feel like myself right now.

"Hey, sweetheart," she says, staring at me with hungry eyes. Looking beyond her to Tyler and George, they give me the thumbs up and wink.

"Why don't you take me upstairs," she says. I try to focus on her face in an attempt to figure out where I know her from. Do we have a class together?

"You can take my room," George says with a smile.

"Let's go," I tell her.

The girl gets up from my lap, and I walk ahead of her, leading her towards the stairs. I get all the way to the top, not bothering to look behind me to see if she's following. I'm sure she is.

I open the second door on the right, letting myself into George's room. Turning on the light, I feel the girl behind me, trying to lift up my shirt.

"Hey," I say, halting her movements.

"Are you ready?" she asks, like she's about to change my life.

Doubtful.

I look at the way she's swaying on her feet. "How much have you had to drink?"

She pouts. "Only a couple of beers. Oh, and two shots!" Although her lips say two, her fingers signal three.

I shake my head. "Get on the bed." She smiles, kicking off her shoes and doing as she's told.

"Under the blankets," I instruct. She looks at me, puzzled, before doing exactly as I say. As soon as she gets comfortable, she yawns.

Good.

I shut off the lights.

"Come join me already," she says, stumbling over her words.

I turn around and open the door. "Not tonight."

"What? Why?"

"I don't sleep with drunk girls," I tell her. I lock the door behind me and walk out. I stand outside the room, hearing her exasperated scream. A few minutes later though, it's quiet.

I walk down the stairs and find Tyler and George in the same spot as I left them.

"Good man!" George says, high-fiving me as I take my seat back on the couch.

Tyler cheers me on too. "Way to handle that shit!"

I don't bother to tell them I didn't sleep with her. I let them think whatever they want.

I'm an asshole, but I'm not about to take advantage of a drunk girl.

I SHOOT THE SHIT WITH THE GUYS FOR A COUPLE OF HOURS, waiting until I'm sober enough to drive. I say my good-

Not the Same

byes and wander outside, sitting in my car for a moment. I don't want to go home. I don't want to be there, to potentially see my mom passed out. Ethan's not there, so I really don't need to go home just yet. As I approach the turn that'll take me back to my house, I wonder if I should just keep driving, to take advantage of this opportunity to have some time away because it doesn't happen often.

I let my street pass me by as I head in the direction of the highway. I drive down the interstate, eventually taking a familiar turn. A few minutes later, I slow the car to a complete stop. Getting out, I cross the road, stepping into a large field. Above me, the sky stretches on forever, the stars burning brightly in a blanket of dark blue silk.

As I pass, I touch the delicate petals of the slumbering flowers. This is where I brought Ethan after we went for ice cream the other day—the day his image of me started to fall apart. *That was my fault.* I wanted him to see the flowers, the open space. I wanted him to run around freely, to do whatever he wanted. To be a child.

As I walk through the field, I remember how much he laughed chasing after me while we played tag. His carefree laugh made me smile in return. It reminded me of how we'd play hide and seek a long time ago. Being here with him helped me forget the bad things even if only for a moment.

Looking around the massive dark field, it seems larger. I continue to walk around it aimlessly and when I find myself in what I think is the middle, I open my arms wide and welcome the breeze.

It's 3am so no one is around. There's nothing in sight for miles.

So, I let go.

I scream at the top of my lungs, letting out all the frustration, the anger, the pain.

I shout until my throat is raw and tears sting my eyes.

I don't know if it'll help but at this particular moment, it feels good. My legs seem to give out then, and I collapse to the ground. Breathing in the fresh night air, I think about the future, of what I want to do with my life—who I want to become.

But just as the breeze causes the flowers to move, my dreams for the future are blown away with it.

4

IT ISN'T ENOUGH—NOT ANYMORE

It's been two weeks since the incident with Richard, and the tension in the house is nearly unbearable. Mom hasn't so much as looked me in the eye since I hurt her precious drug dealer. When I can, and when I know Ethan is in a safe place, I hang out with the guys. Tonight, they decided we'd start celebrating my birthday. They were the only ones that remembered, and when they gave me shot after shot, I downed them.

Now, I'm being driven home, although I can't open my eyes enough to see who it is.

"Go sleep it off, Lincoln," they tell me, reaching across me to open the door. I fall out of the passenger seat of the car, getting on my feet and stumbling up the front steps of my house. I didn't think I was this drunk.

It's actually a miracle I'm walking in the first place. I should be passed out somewhere. I get to the front door and turn the knob. It's locked. Swaying, I pat down my pockets until I find the one with the keys. Behind me, the car that dropped me off drives away, and I briefly wonder who it was. I squint, focusing on the tail lights that move further and further in the distance as another light approaches.

The sun.

Remembering the task at hand, I fish my keys out of my pocket and insert each one into the lock until I find the one that fits perfectly.

Turning the key to the left, I unlock the door and let myself in. All the lights are off, and while the sun peeks through the clouds, the silence I walk into assures me that everyone is still asleep.

I take the steps two at a time, walking past my mother's room, but stopping in front of my little brother's. I know he's sleeping over at yet another friend's house tonight, but I still open the door. Expecting it to be empty, I'm shocked to find a small figure laying asleep in the bed.

Internally, I panic. He wasn't supposed to be home tonight. Knowing he wasn't going to be here was the only reason I allowed myself to go out in the first place. I walk over to his bed, being as careful as possible to not wake him up, and look to see that he's okay.

I don't think my mother would physically hurt him— it's the emotional scarring I fear the most, but I check anyway. Satisfied, I close his door and head over to my own room. Without bothering to even take off my shoes, I drop into bed and give in to sleep—both fatigue and guilt serving as my blankets.

Not the Same

I'M STARTLED AWAKE BY SCREAMING.

"Where are they?" someone yells. The question is too-familiar, and that's when I realize Richard is back.

"I..." my mother says, but I miss whatever else she adds.

"You took them? Are you kidding me!" Richard screams back.

"I needed some. I'm sorry,"

"Where's the money for it?"

"I don't have any," she says, sobbing.

I shake my head, feeling the pounding headache take hold. I get up, going to Ethan's room. He shouldn't have to hear this.

I open his door slightly, finding him still asleep. I look at him for a beat, wishing I could do so much more to protect him.

I turn on the speaker we keep next to his nightstand. George was getting rid of his old one, so I asked him for it to give to Ethan. Ethan was really excited to have something to listen to music on. I was excited to have something that would drown out the noise from just outside his door, like the yelling and screaming that's happening right now.

I find one of his favorite songs on an old iPod I got from Tyler and play it. I don't raise the volume because I don't want to wake him up.

Closing his door, I walk quietly downstairs.

"Get off me!" Richard screams. In the kitchen, I'm disgusted by the scene that greets me. My mother is on her knees, clutching onto Richard's leg for dear life.

She's sobbing, her mascara running down her face.

"Don't leave! I'll get you some money. I promise," she begs.

"Get off!" When she shakes her head, he starts walking towards the living room, dragging her along with him.

"Can you both keep it down," I say in a leveled voice. I don't want to add to the noise, to wake Ethan.

Richard turns around, glaring at me. "Mind your own business, kid!"

"Asshole," I say under my breath. I look down at my mom, but she doesn't even glance my way.

"Fuck off!" Richard says, looking down at her, but his words are directed at me. He pries my mother's hands from his leg, shoving her away so hard she hits the wall with a sickening *thud*.

Fisting Richard's shirt, I get up in his face, aching to start a fight. Again.

"Don't you ever touch her again." I say each word slowly as I wait for him to remember who was begging for air the last time.

"Or what?" he spits back. "What will you do?" He says this with an air of confidence—a smug smile—and I cock my arm back, ready to knock out what's left of his teeth.

I'm stunned when my mom wraps her fingers around my wrist and squeezes. "Stop, Aron."

My eyes dart to her for a second before I turn back to Richard. "Get the hell out of our house and never come back," I tell him. Knowing my mother is still standing right behind me gives me some assurance she's finally seen through his act—can see the evil he brings.

"Don't you dare speak to him that way."

Not the Same

My mother's tone is low—dangerous—and I'm caught off guard; I've never heard her speak like that before. I turn, stunned to see she's talking to me like I'm the enemy.

"He's a piece of shit," I say, trying to get through to her.

She slaps me hard across the face, the sound echoing off the walls.

I close my eyes, taking a deep breath.

Holding back the tears.

Not because of the slap, but because of what it confirms. My mother doesn't give a shit about me. All she cares about is him and his drugs.

"I'll be back later," Richard says with satisfaction in his voice. My mother begs him to stay, but judging by the sound of the door slamming, I think her pleas aren't answered. I stand there, wondering what happened to the woman I used to know.

"Son," she says, her voice small as she turns away from the closed door and looks at me.

With the shake of my head, I begin walking back toward the stairs.

She sniffles. "I'm so sorry," she says, her voice cracking.

Her apology makes me flinch; I'm experiencing déjà vu. Sadly, we've been here before. I glance at her one last time, seeing the regret painted on her face.

Too bad it isn't enough.

Not anymore.

"You're sorry all the time."

5

TEARS FLOW DOWN HER FACE, BUT SHE DOESN'T SAY ANYTHING

"Can we stop for ice cream?" Ethan asks the moment he gets into the backseat of my dad's old car. It's the only thing he left behind the day he walked out on us.

Sometimes I still can't believe it's almost been ten years. I remember it like it was yesterday...

My mom was pregnant with Ethan. She was glowing. I recall her long hair blowing in the wind as she set up a family picnic in the backyard. She wanted to surprise Dad with it when he got home from work. I was seven years old, but I was so excited to get to eat snacks and spend time with Mom and Dad.

To be honest, I was a little jealous that another boy was on the way. I wanted to be the only boy—the only child. I didn't want to share my parents' love. So, I was taking advantage of all the time I could get with them before the baby arrived and took them away from me. I knew how parents got with a new

Not the Same

baby. I compared it to how I got when I got a new toy—the old ones forgotten.

I ran to the door the moment I saw Dad's car pull into the driveway. I eagerly shouted his name, but he didn't hear me. He looked different somehow—he looked sad. I asked him how his day had gone but he ignored me. He just hung his coat, set down his briefcase, and walked straight to the backyard.

I followed behind him until he told me to go upstairs and play.

I begged to go outside, but he said no.

I didn't want to miss out on the food and I wanted to play with them. But my dad made it clear I was to stay inside the house and not come out unless he said so. I was confused. Dad had never talked to me like that before. I wondered if the baby effect had already taken hold; it wasn't even out of her stomach yet. Did they want to be together, just the three of them?

I didn't go up to my room right away. Instead, I stood by the kitchen window, trying to see what was happening in the backyard.

I saw my mother's eyes light up as she stood unsteadily from the blanket, ready to hug him—to welcome him home.

He avoided her kiss, turning his face away.

My mother's eyes were questioning, wondering what was going on. I knew, even at that early age, that she was asking him if something was wrong.

He spoke to her, her eyes watching him intensely. She didn't seem to move until my dad said something that made her cover her mouth with her hand.

Tears began to stream down her face.

She shook her head while Dad just stood there. He didn't try to make the tears stop.

I'd never been mad at my dad before, but he was making my mom cry.

He wasn't supposed to do that.

He walked back into the kitchen, barely glancing at me, and into the living room. Following, I saw him pick up his briefcase.

Approaching cautiously, I asked, "Where are you going, daddy?"

Shrugging on his coat, he looked back at me briefly before opening the door and walking away.

I STILL REMEMBER THE SOUND OF THE DOOR SHUTTING IN my face.

That was the last time I ever heard from him. After he left, things were okay for a few years—Mom was managing—but three years later that all changed. When I was ten, Richard walked into our lives, shaking it up all over again.

"Hello, are you there? Can we pretty please get ice cream?" Ethan asks pulling me from my thoughts. I didn't realize I'd dived so far into my memories.

"Yeah, of course, buddy. We'll stop on our way home," I tell him. Putting the car in drive, I look back at my little brother. Even though I don't remember much else about my father, I remember more than Ethan ever will. He never got to meet our father, has never even seen a photo. My mother erased his memory from our lives that same night.

I mean, she's told me story after story. Dad lost his job. Dad stopped loving her. Dad didn't want to be a dad. Dad was having an affair. She kept giving me reason after reason, excuse after excuse, but the story changed every time so I don't know what to believe.

All I know is that my father wasn't a real man. A real man doesn't walk out on his pregnant wife—on his sons.

Now, I only remember him as the person that caused my mother to make one bad choice after another. I realize it's not entirely his fault, but if it weren't for him leaving us, perhaps she'd be different. Perhaps she'd be okay.

Shaking my head, I push down my thoughts and questions, pull out of the parking lot, and drive toward the ice cream shop.

"Thank you for taking me to get ice cream," Ethan says the moment we get home.

I ruffle his hair. "No problem, buddy."

"We should do that every day," he says with a smile.

Yeah, right. "I'm not getting you ice cream every day. Maybe once a week. We can do ice cream Fridays."

"That works for me," he says with a smirk.

I shake my head when I realize he's played me. "I see what you did there," I tell him proudly. He'll be a great negotiator. I wonder what he'll want to study in the future. I wonder who he'll become.

"You gotta be smarter than that," he says, patting me on the back.

I nod. "I agree. I can't let you play me like that." I take the steps up to Ethan's room two at a time and when I turn back, I see him doing the same. He's emulating me, doing as I do.

Working on that theory, I take the steps one at a time instead, smiling when I see him copying me again.

He wants to be like me, which makes me want to be better. For him.

When we reach the top of the stairs, we walk straight into his room to start on his homework.

"I'm just going to get changed," I tell him. "Be right back."

I leave Ethan to pull out his books while I go to my room and change into something more comfortable. Grabbing the books and notebooks I need for my homework, I walk back towards Ethan's room.

I'm about to open the door to Ethan's room when I hear the sound of water running. I don't think anything of it until I see a small puddle of water in front of my mother's bedroom door.

Swearing under my breath, I set the books down on a small table and walk towards her bedroom instead.

I step into a flooded room, my exasperation increasing.

"Mom?" I call out. "Jennifer?" Maybe she'll answer to that instead. After waiting a few more seconds, I turn the knob and let myself into the bathroom...

Where I find my mother on the floor.

Moving quickly, I shut off the water in the shower then check for my mom's pulse.

It's weak, but it's there.

Not the Same

I shake her to try and wake her up. "Mom?" I glance behind me to make sure the door is shut. I don't want Ethan to come in here. He doesn't need to see this. "Mom!"

She isn't responding.

I look down, finding an empty bottle of Oxy on the floor. There are a few pills scattered around, but the majority are gone.

She must have taken them all.

Shit.

"What do I do?" I ask out loud. I need to get the drugs out of her body. Turning her on her side, I pry open her mouth and push my fingers down her throat until she starts to gag. Convulsing, she throws up, and when she's done, I do it again and again until I feel like there's nothing left in her stomach.

For a few heart-stopping minutes, I don't know whether it's enough…

But then a little color returns to her face and her eyes flutter open.

"Aron?" she says.

"I'm here," I assure her.

With a grunt, I lift her from the floor and help her into the tub.

Still clothed, I run the water, watching it fall over her —washing away the evidence.

She peers up at me and I see the disappointment in her face. It's the same disappointment written on mine.

Confident she can sit up unaided, I grab a few towels from under the sink and begin drying the floor.

"Get me out of here, Aron," she says after a few minutes.

Turning off the water, I towel her dry over her clothes then help her move into her room. Grabbing one of her old nightgowns from her closet, I set it beside her then finish cleaning up the bathroom floor. When I walk out, I find my mother in the same position I'd left her in, her eyes downcast, tears streaming down her face.

"Can you dress yourself?" I ask, the wet towels bundled in my arms.

She doesn't reply, but I'm too angry to try anymore. I walk towards the door.

"I'm sorry," she utters as I turn the knob and let myself out.

Throwing the towels into the wash, I head to my room to change out of my wet clothes before going back to Ethan's room.

"What took you so long?" he asks the moment I walk through the door.

I force a smile. "I couldn't find my notebook."

"You really do need to be smarter," he jokes.

"That I do," I tell him, ruffling his hair. Sitting down in the chair next to him, we work through his homework, and mine, for the rest of the night. I go downstairs to grab him a snack and then some supper. When he falls asleep, I stay in the room with him.

I know even if I try, I won't be able to get any rest tonight.

6

WHO WOULD'VE THOUGHT SHE NEEDED TO HIT ROCK
BOTTOM BEFORE SHE PUSHED HERSELF UP?

"Would you like some eggs for breakfast?" my mother asks me for the second week in a row. Seriously, the second week. I study her for a few minutes, in awe of the progress she's made.

The day after I found her almost lifeless body on the bathroom floor, she apologized to me.

She cried.

She hugged me.

She was angry at herself.

She finally understood what she was doing to us, and while I know that must've been a terrible realization, it's what she needed. Near-death experiences tend to give people the wakeup call they need.

"I'm good, thank you," I tell her.

"Are you sure? You gotta make sure you're eating right for football," she tells me.

I look at Ethan, who's happily eating his scrambled eggs and playing around with his iPod. Although he may not know all the terrible things that have happened, even he can feel that the air is lighter—that we're all happier.

"I'm not on the football team anymore," I tell her, watching her expression fall.

She nods to herself. "It's my fault, right?"

I look over at Ethan. "No," I tell her, but we both know that's a lie.

She rounds the kitchen table, playing with my hair like she did when I was six-years-old. "I'm sorry, baby."

"It's okay."

"No, it's not."

"No, it's not," I agree. "But you're better now." And she is. She hasn't been doing drugs, she's been going to group meetings and Richard hasn't been by. I think things are finally starting to look up for our family. Who would've thought she needed to hit rock bottom before she pushed herself up?

She kisses the top of Ethan's head in the most motherly gesture I've seen in years. "Well, since I'm better now, how about you go back to playing football?" she asks her eyes lighting up.

I shake the idea away. "I don't think that's necessary."

"Do you love it?" she asks and I nod. "Then try it again. I'm sure the coach would let you play. Are you any..." She stops herself before finishing the sentence. She wouldn't know if I'm any good at football because she's never been to any of my games. When I was younger, it was my dad that played with me and taught me but, even then, she never showed up.

"I'll talk to Coach," I answer. I don't want her to be sad. I don't want her to think about her failures, not when

Not the Same

she's doing so well, not when Ethan finally has a mother who's paying attention to him.

"Great! Let me know what he says," she says eagerly. "Are you ready, kiddo?" she asks Ethan.

"Ready for what?" Ethan asks, finally tearing his eyes from his toy.

"School? We gotta get going!" she says, taking the empty plates from the table.

Ethan looks at me then back at Mom. "Aron usually takes me to school..."

"Yeah, I don't mind taking him," I echo. That's sort of been my role for a while and I'll admit it feels odd to be letting her take over. Despite how much progress she's made, I should still be cautious.

"How about you take Ethan and I pick him up?" she suggests and while I want to do both, I decide to give her a chance.

7

I'VE GOTTEN TO SEE MORE AND MORE OF THE WOMAN SHE USED TO BE EVERY DAY

I gave it a couple of weeks before asking the coach if I could be a part of the team again. I wanted to give it time before I left Ethan alone with Mom. I'm ashamed to say I didn't trust her. I didn't believe she was actually better. She'd promised to get better before, failing every time, so I didn't think this time would be any different.

Every day, I waited for the other shoe to drop, but it never did.

It's been months now, and she's still waking up early every morning and having breakfast ready before Ethan and I even wake up. She's been taking him to school every morning and picking him up afterwards.

She hasn't missed a single school pick up. She hasn't so much as been late in picking him up either. Even Ethan is doing better in class.

Last night, I got home after practice and found the two of them asleep on the couch, Toy Story playing in the background.

Not the Same

I'd felt a pang in my chest, pushing it away almost immediately. I knew it was a flash of jealousy because I missed having *that* mom. So, yeah, after realizing she was on the wagon for the long term, I decided to pick up football again.

George taps me on the shoulder as we get ready to play my first game back, a grin splitting his face in two. "Dude! I'm so happy to have you back on the team!"

"Yeah, well, it seems I missed you guys too much to stay away," I tell him with a smile of my own. It feels damn good to be back.

"Dude, we sucked without you. The Backup should never see the field again," Tyler echoes and I laugh. They aren't wrong. The replacement quarterback sucked so much the guys refused to call him by his actual name.

"We'll turn it around," I assure them. I may have missed a couple of games, but nothing could ever be so bad that it can't be fixed. I mean, look at my mom. I never thought she'd reroute her life and be in a good place again, but she is.

"We'd better!" George shouts and one of the other guys high-fives him in response.

"Are we ready for tonight?" I yell, loud enough for all the guys to hear.

They all look at me. "Yes!"

"What are we gonna do?" I shout once again, engaging in the ritual I usually leave for before our game.

I didn't realize how much I'd missed it until this very moment.

"We're gonna win!" they all chant in unison.

"We're gonna what?"

Hitting the lockers, they scream, "WIN! WIN! WIN!"

As soon as the clock runs out, I run straight over to where Ethan and Mom are sitting. I'm experiencing a high unlike ever before. The other team didn't know what had hit them as even our special teams scored. The guys went out there and commanded the field.

Winning this game and doing what I love again isn't the only reason I can't wipe the smile from my face. The high comes from seeing Ethan and my mom in the stands cheering for me. Seeing them motivated me to play the best game of my life. I never thought I wanted someone in my corner. I didn't think I'd appreciate having a parent to hug at the end of the game, but today made me realize I've always wanted all these things—I just never thought they'd be possible.

As I near them, I find them both wearing the school's colors, laughing together, both incredibly happy.

"Hey," I say with a smile.

I feel my mother's delicate hands go around my body as she embraces me. I return her hug like I haven't done in years. "You were so good out there, Aron," she says, holding me at arm's length, pride shining in her eyes. I see a glimpse of the mother I loved so much when I was younger.

Not the Same

"Thanks, Mom!" I reply.

"Way to go, Linc!" Ethan shouts, and I crouch down to hug him too.

I ruffle his hair. "Thanks, buddy!"

Someone pats me on the back, and when I turn around, I see George standing there. "Bro, we're going to have a little celebration at my house!"

Shaking my head, I say, "Nah, I'm good. I'm just gonna go home."

A small celebration for George is code for a huge party.

"You should go celebrate!" my mother says, and I glance back at her.

Shaking my head, I say, "I'm going to hang with Ethan tonight."

"Come on, dude! The whole team's going to be there and you're the quarterback... again. We gotta celebrate and we can't do that without you!" George presses.

Mom looks at Ethan and then at me. Her eyes light up. "How about you go to the party and then tomorrow, you, Ethan and I can have our own celebration."

"Are you sure, Mom?" I ask.

"Of course!"

"Is that okay with you buddy?" I ask Ethan.

He nods. "Yes!" he answers then turns to Mom. "Mom, can we watch Toy Story 2 tonight?"

"Of course we can!"

"Okay, it's settled then," George says and I shake my head.

I give Ethan and Mom a final hug each. "Thanks for coming to watch me play. I'll see you guys later."

8

SHE PROMISED ME

The team is on a roll. Since I started playing over three weeks ago, we've won every game. We may not make it to the championship but we're gonna try. I take a sip of the beer I'm holding as we sit in George's living room celebrating the win.

Feeling my pocket vibrate, I pull out my phone and answer the call. "Linc?" My little brother's voice comes through the other end of the line.

"What's going on?" I ask him, setting the beer bottle on the table in front of me.

"Richard's back and I think he and mom are fighting," he says, his voice cracking. I can tell he's trying not to cry as he sniffles through the phone.

I get up, walking away from the noise of the party. "Where are you?"

"I'm in the closet," he tells me. At least he can't see it. I wish I never had.

I try and school my voice so he doesn't sense the fear that's overtaking me. "Good, stay there," I coach him.

"Aron? I'm scared," he whispers. That little voice—the voice of a child who's gone through so much more than anyone his age should, makes me run in the direction of my car. I should've stayed home. I hate myself for not seeing this happen. Then again, I thought this time she had changed.

"It's okay, buddy; just stay in the closet." I try to push down the anger, fighting the tears that threaten to spill.

I can't believe this is happening again.

"They're screaming now," he tells me. As he narrates each horrible scene, I wish nothing more than to shield him from all of this mess.

"What did you do after the game?" I ask, trying to distract him.

"Mom and I watched Toy Story 2," he says. He pauses then adds, "Something just broke." I take off running toward my car. I'm bumping into people as I move through the crowd, but I don't care. I have to get to my little brother.

"Listen to me, okay? Just stay in the closet and think about what happened in Toy Story. Can you tell me what happened in the movie?"

He starts to tell me his favorite scene as I pry open the driver's side door and get in. I twist the key in the ignition, the engine rumbling to life. Shifting the car into gear, I peel out of the driveway.

I have one focus—to protect Ethan.

And nothing and no one will stand in my way.

Not anymore.

I run every red light, knowing it's not safe, knowing I'm risking not just my life, but others as well.

But I don't care.

I shielded Ethan from as much of this as I could. I've lived my life as his bodyguard, preventing him from seeing the way our mother has been throwing her life away by depending on drugs and making *them* her most important relationship.

At least he got to see the good side of Mom—the doting and caring mother that made him breakfast and packed him snacks for school.

I got the one who walked through the doors every other day with tears in her eyes, promising she'll change after she's given in to the vice once again. I got the version that promised me she'd sober up and return to being the mother I once knew—I guess it didn't stick.

I TAKE A SHARP LEFT ONTO MY STREET, DRIVING AS QUICKLY as I can. The sounds around me are muffled as I let my need to get to Ethan fuel me.

She said things between her and that bastard were over.

She was getting clean. She was trying to find a job, trying to be a better person.

She promised me.

She lied.

9

I THOUGHT THINGS WOULD GET BETTER

Red and blue lights flash behind me, and I know I should stop.

But I don't.

I continue to drive, the lights moving closer and closer before disappearing. Pulling up alongside me, the police officer doesn't even glance my way. Instead, he picks up speed, cutting in front of me sharply. I think for a second that he's going to hit the brakes, causing me to slam into him, but he shows no sign of slowing down.

I take that as my cue to follow him; he'll clear the road so I can reach my destination as quickly as possible.

I dial the number Ethan had used to call me once again, but it goes straight to voicemail.

I keep driving, stunned to see the police are driving in the same exact direction as I am—even turning onto my street.

At the far end, I see a bunch of flashing red and blue lights.

Yanking on the wheel, I pull the car over and jump out. I run towards my house.

Shit.

"Where are you going?" one of the officers standing outside my house yells.

"Stop! Hey! Stop right there!" someone else shouts, but nothing is stopping me.

I reach my front door where I find five more officers barring me from entering my house.

"You can't go in there," one of them says.

Like hell I can't. That's my house. "My brother," I tell them, my tone clipped.

"There's a kid in there?" another cop asks, clearly surprised.

I shove my way past them—*screw the consequences*—and I run straight toward my room, right to the place I know my brother is hiding.

"Ethan," I whisper. I don't want to scare him any more than he is.

I hear ruffling before the closet door opens slightly. "Linc, is that you?" a fragile voice asks and I sigh in relief.

"Yes, E. It's me," I assure him. "You can come out now."

"Are you sure?"

I breathe in deeply, trying to keep my emotions at bay. "Yes, everything's okay now." I don't know if that's true, but he's okay and that's all that matters to me.

He peeks his head out of the closet, looking around. Cautiously, he creeps out of the closet, taking slow steps at first, then quicker ones as he runs into my arms.

I tighten my hold, like I might not see him ever again.

Not the Same

I don't know what I would've done if something had happened to him. "You're okay, buddy."

"We're going to need you two to come with us," someone says from behind us. I look back to see a man in a blue uniform looking down at us. His eyes are filled with pity and that's when I remember the herd of officers outside.

"What happened?" I ask, rising from my crouch.

"We just need to ask you some questions," the officer says, and that's when I realize this is far from over.

"Where are you going?" Ethan asks.

We're down at the station, and I can tell Ethan is getting more and more stressed with what's happening. "I just have to talk to the man from earlier. It'll only take a couple of minutes."

"Is everything okay?" he asks again. I don't know enough to have an answer, and I'm not sure I could tell him even if I did know.

"Yes," I lie once again. "I'll be right back."

"Promise?" he asks and I feel like I'm looking at the younger version of me.

I nod. "I promise."

"Okay," he concedes, trusting me at my word. I'll never leave him behind. I'll never break a promise to him —I won't be like our mother.

A female officer, who's been waiting with us, sets up a puzzle, asking Ethan to join her.

My brother looks at me for confirmation. "Go ahead," I say. "I bet you'll have it finished before I get back."

Ethan bites his bottom lip, considering his options before cautiously sitting down at the table. The officer starts asking him about school and what he likes to do. Like any child would, Ethan finds himself eager to answer all of her questions, the earlier concern erased.

"Do you think we can beat your big brother and get this done before he gets back?" she asks pointing at the puzzle, and Ethan nods enthusiastically.

Confident Ethan will be fine, I leave the room.

"He'll be okay," the escorting officer tells me. "Kids are resilient."

Numbly, I just stare at him. Of course he'd say that. He's probably seen this exact same thing unfold a hundred times over. And that makes me angry. Determined. Regardless of what I have to do, Ethan will be okay. I won't let anything hurt him, or allow anyone to destroy his childhood like mine was.

He shows me into a room. "I'm Officer Alvarez." He extends his hand and I shake it. Gesturing behind him, he says, "And this is Officer Jones. If you could take a seat, please," he adds.

As if I'm not in control of my own feet, I move towards the table, taking a seat. He sits down too, and another cop, who I vaguely remember from my house, walks in and closes the door. I glance around. We're in an interrogation room—a room usually reserved for what I assume are perpetrators. I start to worry whether I'm in trouble.

"Is everything okay?" I ask, feeling the same vulnerability Ethan did.

Not the Same

"It will be," the officer assures me.

"Son, we responded to a call at your home."

In rushing to make sure Ethan was okay, I didn't even give myself a moment to think about what had caused all of the cops to be at my house in the first place. I mean, Ethan told me that Mom and Richard were fighting, but that's not new. They scream and fight and throw shit, but the cops never show.

"Is my mother okay?" I ask. I may not think she's a good mother, but I'm not heartless. She still gave birth to my brother and me. She was, at some point, a decent parent before addiction and Richard consumed her life.

"She's in the hospital," he says.

"What did that bastard do?" I ask, standing up so quickly, my chair tips and falls behind me.

Officer Alvarez stands up too, walking around to pick up my chair. "We responded to a call about a heroin overdose."

"My mother OD'd?" My words come out in a whisper. She was yelling over the phone when Ethan called. How could she have overdosed in the time it took me to get home?

He sets my chair back, nodding at it. I sit. "We were able to bring her back with Narcan."

My mother had died.

"Where's Richard?" I ask.

"Who's Richard?"

I run my fingers through my hair. "My mother's boyfriend." *Who I thought was out of our lives for good.*

"When we showed up at the house, it was just your mother lying on the kitchen floor." The imagery he paints is sure to haunt me. I watch Officer Jones standing silently behind him.

"We received an anonymous call and that's what we responded to," he adds.

Anonymous call my ass. That was Richard, too cowardly to stay and help out the woman he's dealt drugs to for years.

"Son, we have a couple of questions for you," Alvarez says, and I realize I'm the one who's been asking them for the most part.

I nod. Officer Alvarez opens a manila folder and slides a few pictures toward me.

"When we responded to the call, we found these on the kitchen table," he says, tapping the photos with his index finger. I look down and see a few bags of what I know is cocaine and heroin.

"Does your mother do drugs often?" he asks and I consider how I should answer. "Aron, this is important," he presses. "I know you don't want to get your mom in trouble, but she could've died tonight. She needs help, and so do you and your brother."

I nod at the mention of my brother.

"Does she sell them?" he asks.

"I don't think she does. Richard does though," I say, throwing him under the bus. At this moment, I'd literally shove him in front of a moving car myself for all the wreckage he's brought into our lives.

"Do you think your mother is an addict?" he asks and I laugh bitterly. She's been an addict for years now.

"Aron?"

The smile leaves my face. "Yes."

Not the Same

The cop rubs at his beard, looking at me with pity-filled eyes.

"What's going to happen now?" I ask.

He puts the photos back into the folder. "I'm not sure. I don't think your mother will face jail time, but she will have to go to rehab." *Rehab?* I wonder if it'll work. She looked like her old self the last few months. Maybe with help she could be that way permanently.

"The family court judge will likely find that she isn't fit to care for you until she gets through the program and proves she's not endangering her children."

"Not fit to care for us?" I echo. If those words aren't gospel, I don't know what is.

"The court will take you and your brother from her custody."

If the court says she can no longer have us... "Where are we going to go?" I finish my thought out loud.

"Is your father in the picture?"

"I haven't heard from my father in years. He could be dead for all I know."

He purses his lips as if what he just heard is distasteful. "Do you have any extended family? The court may award them temporary custody if they can provide a safe environment for you both." I quiet the thoughts in my head, focusing specifically on where Ethan and I could go. There's no one on my father's side.

"I have an aunt," I tell him. "She's my mother's sister." We used to be really close. She used to take us to her house for the weekends every so often. Then, something happened between her and Mom and all I remember is her leaving our house with tears in her eyes after dropping us off. She did sneak a piece of paper into my pocket that day and told me to call her if I ever need anything, to call her if I ever felt unsafe.

I never did.

I thought things would get better.

I was wrong.

10

WE AREN'T LIVING THE LIVES WE WERE SUPPOSED TO LIVE

"So, what happens now?" Someone asks from right outside the door. I'm sitting inside the same room Ethan and I first were first led to, watching him take one of the smaller race cars from the basket provided by the police, and navigating it through a makeshift track.

"The boys are in there," Officer Alvarez says and my ears perk up.

I look at Ethan, ruffling his hair. "I'll be right back," I say, standing up. If someone is going to talk about what's going to happen to us, I need to be party to it.

I step outside the room, coming face-to-face with Alvarez. Beside him is someone I haven't seen in a while. The woman looks just like my mom—well, the way my mother used to look before the drugs. She's got long dark hair, soft facial features, and she's shorter than me by at least a foot. She turns to me and I'm met with my Aunt Eve's hazel eyes.

"Oh, my goodness," she says, bringing her arms

around me. I don't return her hug—just stand there stiffly.

She must sense my hesitance because she drops her arms instantly. "I haven't seen you for so long."

I nod. "It's been a few years."

"You're all grown up," she says, and I can hear the regret in her voice. I wonder what *she* regrets...

Probably leaving us with my mother.

I wonder if she knew.

"What's going to happen now?" I ask the same question I assume Eve had, shifting my eyes from her to Alvarez, who's watching the encounter with interest.

He scratches his head. "The Department of Children, Youth, and Families will likely allow your aunt to take you and Ethan home if she–" He stops and I can tell he feels uncomfortable "––if she wants to."

"To our house?" I ask.

"No. You'd be going back to her house."

I wait for her to object, for her to say she can't possibly let us into her home. I'm waiting for her to shut the door on the whole idea and for Ethan and me to be left on our own, like it's always been.

Instead, she says, "Of course!" There's not an ounce of hesitation. "What do I have to do to take them with me? Where's Ethan?" she asks, finally noticing his absence.

"You just have to fill out a form and we should have the approval soon," Alvarez says.

"Ethan is playing with some toys right now," I add, answering her question.

She looks toward the door I'd come out of a few

minutes ago, worry creasing her brow. "Does he know what's happening?"

I shake my head. "He doesn't have a clue. I didn't know how to tell him. I don't *want to* tell him, not until I know what's going on."

Not until I figure out how to protect him.

"Okay, I'll go see him in a few. I want to get all the paperwork done so we can leave this place as quickly as possible," she says, looking around at the police station. How is it possible that she seems so put together when my mother is falling apart?

"What will happen after?" I press. I know I've asked similar questions before but it's still so unclear.

Eve brings her hand to my cheek, something my mother did to me too. "I'll figure it all out and then we'll talk about it at the house. Don't worry about it."

I know she thinks telling me to not worry is what I need right now, but that couldn't be further from the truth. I need answers.

Sensing my hesitation, she adds, "It's going to be okay, Aron. I promise."

Her words don't comfort me though.

Too many promises have been broken; I don't think I believe in them anymore.

"Aron?" I spin around to find Ethan at the door.

Kneeling in front of him, I look up at him and ask, "What's up, buddy?"

"I want to show you something!" he says excitedly I follow him inside, glancing behind me once and nodding at Eve. I'm giving her permission to go and figure it all out. In the meantime, I'll figure out how to break it to

Ethan that we'll be hanging out with our aunt for a little bit.

As we drive to Eve's house, I take in my surroundings. Gone is the neighborhood I've lived in my entire life. Instead, we find ourselves in a place that looks completely different. All the houses here look the same. The grass is green, the houses are painted white, and there are kids playing without fear out in the yard.

We drive by a house and see a family having a barbecue with what I assume are their friends. They all laugh and chat, completely carefree.

I guess the grass really is greener on the other side.

I look away.

This is too normal. It only reminds me that our childhood was far from perfect.

We aren't living the lives we were supposed to live.

The car comes to a stop a few minutes later, and Ethan practically jumps out. Taking off my seatbelt, I open the door, and walk out after him. Oddly, he hasn't asked too many questions about the fact that we aren't returning home.

He did ask what would happen to Mom and what we were doing. I told him we were going to be spending some time with our aunt. He was confused for about two minutes before Eve told him she had a game console at home. Then all his worries were forgotten. I wish I could forget that easily.

Following Eve, we walk into the house and she gives

Not the Same

us a quick tour. It has been so long since the last time we were here, I barely remember it. Her house is really nice—not extravagant, but still spacious and comfortable. It looks like a home but I can tell it's empty. She shows us pictures of her husband and pictures of her and my mother when they were little.

I did notice there aren't any pictures of any kids—not even us.

Ethan asks about her husband—our *uncle*—and I knew he'd passed away by the look in her eyes. She wiped a tear away then smiled.

"He's been gone for a couple of years now."

"I'm so sorry," I say, but Eve shrugs.

"We had a wonderful life together."

Pushing her shoulders back, she directs us up the stairs, guiding us to what will be our rooms.

"This will be your room," she says, and Ethan and I both look inside.

She opens the door wider. "Go inside!" she says, excitedly. And in that moment, I can tell she's happy we're here with her despite the circumstances that brought us to her door.

"This is so cool!" Ethan yells, walking inside and going straight for one of the toy cars sitting on the floor. "Can I play with this?" he asks, pointing at a red Mustang.

"It's all yours," she says with a smile as Ethan sits on the floor and starts pushing the car from side to side.

"You didn't have to," I tell her.

She places her hand on my shoulder. "I bought that for him last Christmas. I know I wasn't around much—well, at all—but I've wanted to be. I've bought you guys a birthday and Christmas present every year for the last few years," she says, shocking me completely. She takes a deep breath before adding, "I should've tried harder."

"I—" I start, trying to ease some of her guilt but she stops me once again.

"Let's go see your room."

"You have your own room too?" Ethan asks, looking up from his place on the floor.

Eve nods excitedly. "Yes he does!" She walks out of the room and I follow. Ethan trails behind his, his toy car clutched in his hand. He cuts in front of me, impatient to see what the other room looks like.

"Wow, this one is so much bigger than mine!" he says.

"He's a lot bigger than you are," Eve says gently. "I don't think he'd fit in your bed."

Ethan laughs. "Right? His feet would be hanging off the mattress."

"Yes, they would!" Eve replies, ruffling his hair.

I look around the room, and then look at Eve with Ethan. I don't want him to get too attached to her even though I know he will. We don't know what's going to happen to us next. We don't even know if Eve will want to keep us or if we'll have to go back to our mother.

The only thing I do know is that it's Ethan and me.

Always.

11

I FOUND MYSELF HITTING ROCK BOTTOM

We drive over to the courthouse in silence. Aunt Eve's holding the steering wheel too tightly, her knuckles turning white. For the past six weeks, she's welcomed Ethan and I into her home, voracious in her need to know everything about us. For the first time in seven years, I've actually felt cared for.

I glance over my shoulder at Ethan sitting in the back, distracted by playing with a tablet Eve got him. I'm not sure he's aware of what's going to happen today, and that's just the way I want to keep it.

He looks up as we pull up to a stop in front of an imposing stone building. "What's that?" he asks curiously.

"That's a courthouse."

"Like on TV?" he asks, talking about a show he and Eve started watching last week. She's been really good with him, fielding whatever questions I find myself

153

unable to answer. She's been caring for him like he was her own son—like we both were.

I nod. "Yes."

"What are we doing here?"

I pause to think about what to say, but Eve beats me to it. "We just have a few things to take care of. You'll get to hang out in a room with a bunch of games while your brother and I run a quick errand," she says.

I look at her and she sees the question in my eyes. "I called the court. He doesn't have to be in the room so he gets his own for him to play," she says in a hushed voice.

"Thank you," I mouth to her. I'm grateful she too understands the importance of shielding Ethan.

"Don't mention it," Eve says, resting her hand on mine.

"Do you think you can do that?" the judge asks my mother. I sit next to Eve, who's nervously playing with her hands. I find myself on the edge of my seat, waiting to see what my mother will say next, hanging on her every word.

"Do you think you can do that, Mrs. Lincoln?" the judge asks once again. Her last name isn't Lincoln. It's Robertson. She went back to her maiden name after she and Dad divorced. I think I let my mind hold on to this fact because I'm scared to focus on what's happening now —on what she will say.

"Ah..." my mother starts. The judge waits for her response impatiently, and so do the rest of us.

Not the Same

"Are you willing to follow the necessary steps to get to see your kids again?" she presses.

My mother looks down, then turns to look towards the back of the room. Her gaze meets her sister's then travels to me. "I don't think..." she starts and although I think she's talking to the judge, her eyes are still fixed on me.

The judge exhales loudly. "Could you speak more loudly and direct your response to me?"

My mom pries her eyes away from mine and turns towards the judge. "I don't think I'm... I think they'd be better off staying with their aunt," she answers and the small part of me that held onto the hope that my mother loved us—cared about us—disappears. When she says *we'd* be better off without her, I know she means *she* would be. She doesn't even refer to Eve as her sister—just our aunt.

I stopped looking up to my mother for a very long time now. I just never thought I'd get as far as wishing she wasn't my mother at all.

"Okay then, it's final. Mrs. Lincoln—"

"Robertson," I correct the judge. The court sheriff stares at me and I know it isn't protocol to speak out of turn. To everyone in the room, I'm just an audience member, but I'm not. I'm waiting for the judge to determine what will happen to my brother and me. I'm waiting for her to determine what happens to the rest of my life.

"Pardon me, Ms. Robertson," the judge corrects herself and signals for the sheriff to stand down. She continues, unbothered by my interruption. "I'm inclined to agree with the State in that you are not fit to be a parent. I will, therefore, award full custody of Aron Lincoln and Ethan Lincoln to their aunt, Eve Stephens. It is my sincere hope that you acknowledge the importance of family and take the necessary steps to rehabilitate yourself so that hopefully—one day—you can earn their forgiveness. I sentence you to sixty days of rehabilitation as an outpatient at the Butler Facility. I'll warn you that you should take the program seriously. I don't want to see you in my courtroom ever again. If I do, I will not be as lenient."

I stand up, clearing my throat. "Can I have a moment with her?" I ask the judge. "Please?" In my periphery, I see the sheriff walking in my direction, but that doesn't deter me.

Eve slips her hand into mine, giving it a squeeze. I smile down at her.

"I just want to say a few things to her," I add.

I'm shocked when she says, "You have five minutes. Sheriff, bring him and the Defendant over to the jury deliberation room."

I nod my thanks, and as I pass the bench, she says, "Five minutes, son."

The sheriff ushers me into the deliberation room and another sheriff brings my mother along.

"We'll be right outside the door," one of the sheriffs says to me. I nod. This won't take long.

With the door shut, it's silent between us. My mom looks at me, her spirit broken.

"I'm—" she starts, but I hold my hand up to stop her. "No. You don't get to speak now. I have something to say to you, and then we're done. You...you've been playing on the edge for so long and I've kept trying to save you from falling. Yet the only one that ended up almost drowning was me." My eyes are locked on hers, perhaps for the last time. "In an attempt to keep your head above the water, I found myself hitting rock bottom."

I pause and take a deep breath. "I'm done trying to be your lifeguard. I can't take on the role of being your parent too."

A tear slides down her face, but I say what I need to before I lose the strength.

"You were supposed to be the parent. I was supposed to be the child—not the other way around. You had so many chances to change, to seek help. You could've turned your life around, for yourself, for us, but you turned each of them down.

"You were given a chance by a judge to get your children back. All you had to do was get clean, attend rehab —*stay* sober..." I laugh, because it's the only thing I can do to stop myself from crying. I'm glad Ethan isn't here to see this, to be *scarred* by this. "You decided it wasn't worth it. You decided *we* weren't worth it."

She sobs audibly.

"Today, I'm giving up on you too. I'm choosing to save *Ethan and I* this time."

Her shoulders begin to shake as she tries to hold in her tears. I want to comfort her because that's my instinct, but I won't. Instead, I straighten my spine, turn away, and walk out of the room.

12

MOM BROKE HER PROMISE. THERE'S NO WAY I'M BREAKING MINE

I stumble in the dark, searching for the keys Eve gave me two weeks ago. I put my hands in my pockets, emptying them. I hear the keys fall to the floor, so I bend down to start searching for them.

It's dark outside.

Everything around me is spinning.

I don't even remember what happened today. I started at a new school a couple of weeks ago.

It's weird being the new kid, but it's not terrible. When the coach heard I'd played football for my old school, he asked me to join the team. The guys welcomed me so easily, deciding I needed to be inducted into the team properly. So after practice today, we partied.

We partied so hard I'm still on my hands and knees looking for my keys.

How the hell did I even get to Eve's house in the first place?

Yes! I finally find my keys and stand up, wobbling slightly.

I must have had close to twenty shots. I don't even recall what happened for most of the night.

After dropping the keys three different times, I finally get the door to open.

I walk in as quietly as possible, trying not to wake anyone up. I close the door slowly but it slams shut instead. I look up at the stairs, hoping no one's heard it. I take a few steps in that direction, intending to go upstairs, but at the last second, I reroute into the kitchen for a glass of water.

After gulping it down, I return to the stairs, stumbling and tripping all the way up.

I pass Eve's door, and then Ethan's. I keep walking and just as I turn the knob on my bedroom door, I hear small steps coming in my direction.

"What are you doing?" Ethan asks me, rubbing his eyes.

I can't believe I woke him up. "I was just getting some water."

He frowns. "You're drunk," he says and his words sober me up instantly.

"I—I had a few drinks tonight," I tell him. It breaks me to see the disappointment in his eyes.

"You're turning into Mom," he says and I feel like I've been punched in the face. "You think just because you're older than me that I don't realize what's going on, but I know more than you think. And you're turning into *her* now. I thought you were better than that. I thought you loved me more than that," he says and I feel a tear slide down my face.

I can't believe I allowed myself to get sucked down

this hole. I'm reaching rock-bottom now. I'm becoming the monster I fought against so fiercely.

"I'm sorry," I say, cringing to hear the words coming out of my mouth. That's something else Mom used to say. I feel like a bucket of cold water has been thrown on me.

He comes closer to me and I sit on the floor. "You're right," I add.

"Why?" he asks, sitting down in front of me

"I was at a party," I tell him.

He shakes his head. "This isn't the first time," he says, calling me out on it.

I thought no one had realized it.

I thought no one saw...

I thought I'd been successfully hiding it.

I take a deep breath and look at him in the eyes. "I think I was trying to cope with the change," I tell him, and once again, I remind myself of our mother.

"That's not a good way to cope," he tells me, repeating the same words I told my mom.

I suddenly understand the meaning of self-loathing.

Is this how my mother felt?

I nod. "You're right. I promise you, I'll never do it again."

"How do I know you'll keep your promise? Mom never did," he says, and those words reveal more to me than he thinks. He knows more than I ever thought he did. Even with how much I tried, it seems I couldn't shield him from it all.

"Because I'm your brother and I'll always look out for you. I've never broken a promise I've made to you before, right?"

Not the Same

"Right," he says.

"I won't start now." I look him in the eye when I say those words so he knows I mean it.

He nods, accepting what I've said like I did with Mom many times before. The only difference is, Mom broke her promise. There's no way I'm breaking mine.

"Don't beat yourself up too much," Eve says, walking into the kitchen the next morning. She goes over to the fridge and pours herself a glass of orange juice then takes a seat in front of me.

"Did you hear?" I ask, putting the Tylenol in my mouth and taking a sip of my water to wash it down.

She nods. "I didn't mean to. I woke up to…"

"The sound of me stumbling up the stairs," I supply.

She takes a sip of her juice. "Well, yes. I wanted to make sure you were alright. I opened the door slightly and found your brother talking to you."

"I didn't see you," I tell her. I'm ashamed she saw me like that too.

"I was going to come out and talk to you, but I think you needed to hear it from Ethan."

I set my drink down. "I never wanted him to see me that way."

"I know, sweetheart," she says, reaching out and taking my hand. "But he was the only one who was going to get through to you."

"I don't know why I did it," I tell her honestly.

She gets up from her chair and comes around the

table, taking a seat beside me. Touching my shoulder, she says, "I know why."

"Why?"

"You've been taking care of your brother, and even your mom, for the last couple of years. From what I heard about her boyfriend," she says, and I flinch at the reminder of him, "he wasn't the best guy either. I'm sure you had to deal with a lot from him too."

I nod, and she continues, "You never had a chance to rebel. You never got to yell back at her. You never got to act out because you had to look out for Ethan. I think when you got the chance to finally fight back, you did."

"By getting drunk?" I ask, mad at myself.

"By getting so drunk you'd forget you're hurting," she says and it makes sense. It also makes me understand a little of why Mom did drugs. I guess she wanted to forget too.

That didn't make it right though.

"That's not a good enough reason."

"No, it's not. If you do it again, you may force me to ground you," she says, laughing.

I look at her, not quite smiling. "That'd be a first..."

"I don't think I have to resort to that because I don't think you'll do it again."

"I won't."

She nods, resolute. "A drink here and there is fine. Just don't use alcohol to cope with your emotions—or drugs either. It didn't work for your mom."

"And it won't work for me either. You don't have to worry. I won't do it again."

"Good. Now, breakfast?"

Not the Same

I nod. "Need some help?"

She smiles broadly. "I'd love some."

Together, we make pancakes, eggs, and bacon. A few minutes later, Ethan runs down the stairs. He appears at the kitchen door, climbing up onto one of the stools at the counter.

"It smells so good!" he says, taking one of the pieces of bacon from the plate.

"Hey, wait for us!" Eve says.

"Sorry!" he smiles at her as he takes a bite of bacon.

"The rest is ready! Let's all sit and eat," I announce.

Eve places the large plate of pancakes on the table and I grab the eggs, setting them beside the other plate. I grab the juice from the fridge and cups from a cabinet, setting one in front of Ethan and I pour him a drink.

"Hey, buddy, I just wanted to say sorry again. I wasn't the kind of person I should've been last night. It won't happen again." I don't want to pretend last night didn't happen. I just want to make sure he knows it was the last time.

"I know it won't. People make mistakes, Aron. Mom made some, I know that too. And one day, she'll come back and we'll forgive her," he says, filling his plate with food.

"Right," I reply.

"Oh, I have a surprise for both of you!" Aunt Eve says, jumping up from her seat. We both look at her, wondering what's got her so excited. "Well, don't just stand there, come on!" she says, urging us to follow her.

We walk over to the door that leads to the garage. She opens it and we look inside.

There are two cars—hers and then another one so covered in dust, it'd take a few hours to clean it by hand.

"Ta-da!" she screams excitedly.

"Do you need us to wash that?" Ethan asks and we both laugh.

"No, silly! This car is for Aron. I know you used an old one when you lived at home and, well, you have to get to and from school."

I stare at her, my mouth hanging open.

I feel Ethan tug at my shirt and I look down to see him staring at me with huge eyes. "What's up?" I ask.

"Do you think she got me a car too?" he says, sounding as hopeful as ever. Eve and I laugh.

"No, I didn't get you a car too. But I thought maybe you and Aron could share this one? He could use it to take you to school every once in a while, when he doesn't have football practice. He could even take you out for ice cream!" she says and Ethan's eyes light up at the idea.

"Are you sure?" I ask, still unable to believe she'd do this for us.

"Yes. It's been in here for a couple of years now, collecting dust. I think you boys can put it to good use."

I walk towards her and give her a hug. She tenses up briefly and I know she's as surprised as I am at the gesture. Then she hugs me back.

"I'm so happy you boys are with me," she says, her voice breaking. "I know it wasn't an ideal situation but I'm happy you're here."

Ethan wraps his small arms around us. "We're glad to be here with you, Aunt Eve," he says.

"You're family," I tell her, and I mean it. She may not

have been someone we grew up with, or got to see every day, but when things got tough, she showed up. She didn't question it. She didn't make up excuses. Instead, she opened her home to us—she opened her heart.

The least we can do is open ours.

EPILOGUE

SHE MATTERS TO ME.

It's a new year and things are looking well. We haven't heard anything from our mother, but I think that's for the better. We're starting to develop a new routine, Ethan's making new friends, and things are good. We're happy. If anyone had asked me last year if I thought things could turn out this way—the answer would've been no.

But Ethan and I were given a second chance. Eve has filled the role of loving parent in just a few months—something my mother failed at for years.

My new school isn't so bad either. Football has been my refuge from all the changes in my life and I'm taking full advantage of every opportunity. Eve wants me to go to college too—it's not something I've allowed myself to think about too much, but it's in the back of my mind.

Tonight, is yet another first. I'm at the homecoming dance—not because I want to, but because as the quarterback of the team, I'm obligated to. I'm also here at Eve's insistence. The ability to start over is not one many people get, and I'd be an idiot to give up on it.

I pull into the student lot, parking my car next to the same motorcycle I normally do, surprised to see it here in the first place. I didn't think she was the kind of girl to come to the homecoming dance. Seeing Dimah every morning has become my daily routine. Maybe one day, I can actually get her to remove her headphones and talk to me.

I walk the short distance to the gymnasium, shifting uncomfortably under the weight of my sports jacket. Unfortunately, it's a requirement of homecoming for football players.

Letting myself into the gym, I find streamers and banners everywhere.

I walk towards one of the tables and pour myself a cup of punch. I take a sip, spitting it back into the cup. It's been spiked and not even with good alcohol.

I opt for a water bottle instead and stand awkwardly at the side of the room, scanning it. I don't realize I'm searching for something until I find it. She stands across the room from me, shadowed and invisible. She's wearing ripped dark jeans and a black sweatshirt, completely different from all the dresses and skirts every other girl is wearing.

She looks around the room then back down at her feet. My gaze is forced away from Dimah when a group of girls come to stand directly in front of me. I look at them expectantly, waiting to see what they want.

"Hey, Aron," one of them says with a sultry smile.

"Hi," I respond.

"You look great!" another one adds.

"Thanks."

One of them—one of the cheerleaders—steps into the line of my body, resting her hand on my chest. "If you ever need anything, let me know," she says with a wink.

When I don't say anything in response, the group takes their cue to leave. In less than a year, I think I've become a different person. I'm wholly focused on getting through high school, going to college, and providing for my brother.

I don't need girls to distract me. I don't need alcohol to drown out my thoughts—my memories. I just need to work hard and take the good with the bad.

When my eyes return to Dimah, I find that she's no longer there. I scan the room—searching for her and catching a glimpse of her leaving the gym.

Instinctively, I follow her, avoiding anyone who tries to stop me.

Out in the hall, I hear her thank someone.

"Whatever," the guy says, snatching the cash from her hand and shoving it into his pocket. He pulls out a joint and hands it to her.

"What the fuck?" I say under my breath.

Dimah's head jerks up then, her eyes widening when she sees me. Spinning on her heel, she hurries out the door.

Enraged, I stalk to Randall—one of the guys on the baseball team, shoving him against the closest locker. "What *the fuck* do you think you're doing?" I fist his shirt, slamming him back into the wall of metal behind him.

"Dude, what the hell?" he asks, confused.

Not the Same

I sneer at him. "Did you just sell her drugs?"

"Yeah, you want some?" he jokes.

"Fuck no," I spit back. "If I ever see you selling that shit on school grounds—" I pause. "If I ever *hear* about you selling drugs to students at all, I'll make sure you get expelled."

"It's just weed," he reasons.

I look at him for a moment longer, feeling him squirm under my hold. "If I hear you're selling this shit again, then getting expelled will be the least of your problems." After a beat, he nods. Shoving him away, I watch him run back down the hall, disappearing through the gymnasium doors.

I take a deep breath, waiting for the anger to subside. When I feel like I'm calm enough, I walk outside, where I see Dimah leaning against the wall near the trash can. The end of the joint glows red as she inhales deeply.

Making sure to keep my voice neutral, I finally say something to her.

"What's a pretty girl like you doing smoking that shit?" I ask, hoping I can convince her not to go down this road. This isn't who she is, or who I think she is, anyway. I find myself too invested in her. I linger nervously, hoping she'll give me the time of day despite knowing she has no idea who I am.

I wait for her answer because it matters to me.

Because for some damn reason I cannot fully comprehend, *she* matters to me.

A WORD FROM GG'S REC ROOM

If You're Struggling Remember...

"Cry a little, let your feelings out, and then look around at what you have accomplished and hold on to that because You Are You and You Are Awesome!! Life sucks, yes, but there is always something to look forward to." – *Cynthia V.O.*

"With every negative you notice, find two positives to counter it. You're worth more than the insidious voice inside says you are. You are Enough." – *Courtney S.*

"Cry when you feel it. Remember everyone has insecurities, but remember you're most valued. If one must move on, grieve, but then tell yourself that life is full of new beginnings. Love yourself because God created you with love." – *Christina G.*

A Word from GG's Rec Room

"Be happy with yourself. Doesn't matter what anyone says, make yourself happy before all others." – *Cynthia C.*

"You are beautiful just the way you are! Don't compare yourself to others. Rather compare yourself today with who you were yesterday, a week ago, or a year ago, and see how far you have come. You are enough! The only people's expectations you have to meet are your own. If someone decides to pass on you, it is not a reflection of you but of them and their insecurities. Be you! You are the only you and the world needs you otherwise you wouldn't be here! So, throw your shoulders back, hold your head up, and let 'em hear you roar!" – *Rachel R.Y.*

"It's okay to cry and let it out. Then, stand up, wipe your face, and keep going because you are beautiful and you are worth it!" – *Samantha S.*

"What would you say to a friend who was feeling the way you are? Would you allow your friend to beat themselves up? Talk badly about themselves? You are important too. Use those words on yourself." – *Jennifer G.*

"It's okay to love yourself." – *Dee S.*

"You are strong. You are beautiful. You are smart. You are enough. Don't let those who have you brought you down continue to do so. Take back the power from those who hurt you. Find yourself. Love yourself." – *Author Gianna Gabriela*

ABOUT THE AUTHOR

Gianna Gabriela is a small town girl living in the Big Apple. Gianna's always been a writer. Growing up, she would write poems, speeches, and even songs. Still, one day she woke up with a pressing need to write a book. She heeded the desire and now writes stories featuring the brooding heroes you want and the strong heroines you need.

Keep up to date - sign up for Gianna's newsletter

Need more?
Here's what to read next...

Bragan University Series

Better With You (Book #1)
Fighting For You (Book #2)
Falling For You (Book #3)
Better With You, Always (Book #4)

COMING SOON
Waiting For You (Book #5)
Finally With You (Book #6)

The Not Alone Novellas

Not the End (Book #1)
Not the Same (Book #2)

COMING SOON
Not Alone (Book #3)

Stand-Alone

Just Because of You
I Fell First